Liesl & Po

'*Liesl & Po* by Lauren Oliver brings much-needed magic to
an increasingly neglected age group . . . there are some
exquisitely drawn characters . . . it's books like this, with
its classic quest plot, intertwined with lyrical metaphysics,
that can set a child up for life.'
Sunday Telegraph

'An absolute delight . . . The story is packed with mystery,
murder, adventure, humour and magic, but above all it is
a beautiful evocation of loss, tempered by the gradual
blossoming of friendship, trust and hope. Although aimed
at younger readers, the lightness of touch and the tenderness
of the message could make grown men weep.'
Daily Mail

'A gorgeous story – timeless and magical . . . For me, this book
was like a ride in a sleeping car on a fabulous train, one with
deep, plush upholstery, shining brass window latches, and
secret compartments, one where the bed slides out soundlessly
and the sheets are not too new but not too old, and where
small amazing cakes arrive regularly on lacquered trays while
the night rushes by outside, the moon always visible.'
Rebecca Stead, Newbery winner for *When You Reach Me*

L&P

....

....

NAME

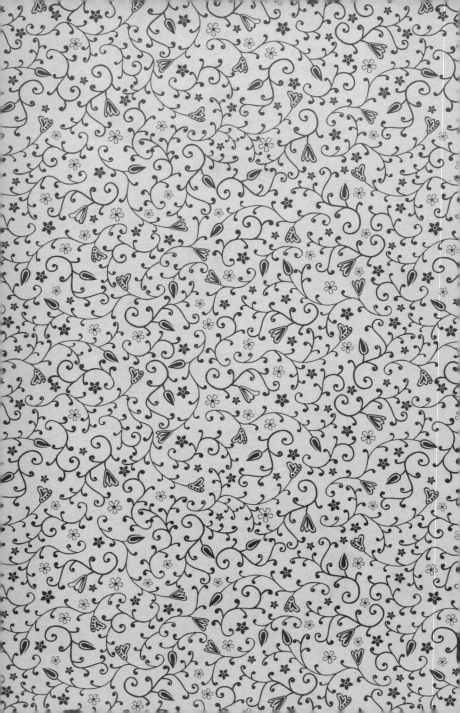

Liesl & Po

LAUREN OLIVER

ILLUSTRATED BY
KEI ACEDERA

HODDER

To Ana and Jack,

and to their children,

Jack, Walter, Lucia, and Freddie—

Inspiration, too,

grows from even the hardest places.

PART I

ATTICS & ACCIDENTS

ONE

ON THE THIRD NIGHT AFTER THE DAY HER FATHER DIED, LIESL SAW THE GHOST.

She was lying in bed in the uniform gray darkness of her small attic room when in one corner the shadows seemed to crimp, or flex, and suddenly standing next to her wobbly desk and three-legged chair was a person about her height. It was as though the darkness was a sheet of raw cookie dough and someone had just taken a cookie cutter and made a child-sized shape out of it.

Liesl sat up, alarmed.

"What are you?" she whispered into the darkness, even though she knew it was a ghost. Normal people do not appear out of darkness, nor seem to be made of liquid shadow. Besides, she had read about ghosts. She read a lot in her little attic room. There was not much else to do.

"Po," the ghost said. "My name is Po."

"Where did you come from?" Liesl asked.

"From the Other Side," the ghost said, as though it were obvious, as though he were saying "from downstairs," or "from Oak Street," or some other place she knew.

"Are you a girl or a boy?" Liesl was wearing the same thin nightshirt she had been wearing since Tuesday, when her father died, and it occurred to her that if the ghost was a boy, she should cover up.

"Neither," the ghost replied.

Liesl was startled. "You have to be one or the other."

"I don't have to be anything," the ghost replied, sounding irritated. "I am what I am and that's all. Things are different on the Other Side, you know. Things are . . . blurrier."

"But what did you used to be?" Liesl pressed. "You know . . . *before*?"

Po stared at Liesl for a while. At least, she thought the ghost stared at her. It didn't really have eyes, exactly. Just two folds of even deeper darkness where its eyes might be.

"I don't remember," it said finally.

"Oh," Liesl said. Next to Po, an even smaller portion of darkness seemed to crimp and flex, and then there was a noise in the corner, a cross between the meow of a cat and the yip of a small dog. "And what's *that*?" Liesl asked.

Po looked toward the place where its feet had once been. "That's Bundle."

Liesl sat forward. She had never had any kind of pet, not even when her father was alive and well, which was ages and ages ago, before he met Augusta, Liesl's stepmother. "Is it yours?"

"Nothing belongs to anyone on the Other Side," Po said. Liesl thought the ghost sounded superior. Then Po added, "But Bundle comes with me wherever I go."

"Is it a dog or a cat?" The little ghost-pet was now making a kind of purring noise in the back of its throat. It slid silently across the room and stared up at Liesl. She could just make out a shaggy head of untrimmed shadow, and two pointed bits of darkness that could have been ears, and two stripes of pale silver moonlight that looked like eyes.

"I told you," Po said, "it isn't one or the other. It's just Bundle. On the Other Side——"

"Things are blurry, I know," Liesl cut in. She was quiet for a moment, and then seemed struck by an idea. "Are you here to haunt me?"

"Of course not," Po said. "Don't be stupid. We have

better things to do with our time." Po hated the impression that living people had of ghosts. It hated their idea that ghosts could find nothing better to do than hang around in basements and abandoned warehouses, jumping out at people.

The Other Side was a busy place—as busy, if not busier, than the Living Side. They ran parallel, the two worlds, like

two mirrors sitting face-to-face, but normally Po was only dimly aware of the Living Side. It was a swirl of colors to the ghost's left; a sudden explosion of sounds to its right; a dim impression of warmth and movement.

True, Po could move back and forth between sides, but it rarely chose to. In all the length of its death, Po had only been back once or twice. Why would it go to the Living Side more often? The Other Side was full of wraiths and shadows moving and jostling; and endless streams of dark water to swim in; and vast depths of cloudless night skies to fly in; and black stars that led into other parts of the universe.

"Well, what are you doing in my room, then?" Liesl demanded, folding her arms. She was annoyed that the ghost had called her stupid, and had decided that if Po was going to be difficult, she would be too.

The truth was that Po wasn't exactly sure why it had appeared in Liesl's room. (Bundle was there, of course, because Bundle went everywhere Po went.) Over the past few months Po had seen a dim light appear at the edges of its consciousness at the same time every night, and next to that light was a living one, a girl; and in the glow of that light the living girl made drawings. And then for three nights the light had not appeared, nor had the glow, nor had the drawings, and Po had been wondering why when—*pop!*—Po had been ejected from the Other Side like a cork popping out of a bottle.

"Why did you stop drawing?" Po asked.

Liesl had been temporarily distracted from thinking about her father. But now she remembered, and a heavy feeling came over her, and she lay back down in her bed.

"Haven't felt like it," she answered.

Po was suddenly at her bedside, just another shadow skating across her room.

"Why?"

Liesl sighed. "My father is dead."

Po didn't say anything.

Liesl went on, "He was sick for a very long time. He was in the hospital."

Po still didn't say anything. Bundle raised itself up on two hind legs of shadow and seemed to look at Liesl with its moonlight eyes.

Liesl added, "My stepmother wouldn't let me see him. She told me—she told me he did not want me to see him like that, sick. But I wouldn't have minded. I just wanted to say good-bye. But I couldn't, and I didn't, and now I won't ever see him again." Liesl felt a tremendous pressure pushing at the back of her throat, so she squeezed her eyes shut and spelled the word *ineffable* three times in her head, as she always did when she was trying not to cry.

Ineffable was her favorite word. When Liesl was very small, her father had often liked to sit and read to her: real grown-up books, with real grown-up words. Whenever they encountered a word she did not know, he would explain to her what it meant. Her father was very smart; a scientist, an inventor, and a university professor.

Liesl very clearly remembered one time at the willow tree, when he turned to her and said, "Being here with you makes me ineffably happy, Lee-Lee." And she had asked what *ineffable* meant, and he had told her.

She liked the word *ineffable* because it meant a feeling so big or vast that it could not be expressed in words.

And yet, because it could not be expressed in words, people had invented a word to express it, and that made Liesl feel hopeful, somehow.

"Why did you want to say good-bye to him?" Po asked at last.

Liesl opened her eyes and stared. "Because—because—that's what you do when people are going away."

Po went silent again. Bundle coiled itself around the place Po's ankles had once been.

"People on the, um, Other Side don't say good-bye?" Liesl asked incredulously.

Po shook its shadow-head. "They push. They mutter. Sometimes they sing. But they don't say good-bye." It seemed to consider this for a second. "They don't say hello, either."

"That seems very rude," Liesl said. "People always say hello to one another *here*. I don't think I would like the Other Side."

The ghost in front of her flickered a bit around the shoulders, and Liesl assumed it was shrugging. "It's not that bad," Po said.

Suddenly Liesl sat up again excitedly, forgetting all about the tiny nightshirt she was wearing and the fact that Po was a maybe-boy. "My father's on the Other Side!" she exclaimed. "He must be there, with you! You could take him a message for me."

Po faded in and out uncertainly. "Not all of the dead come this way."

Liesl's heart dropped back into her stomach. "What do you mean?"

"I mean . . ." Po flipped slowly upside down, then righted itself. The ghost often did this when it thought. "That some of them go straight on."

"On *where*?"

"On. To other places. To Beyond." When it was irritated, the ghost became easier to see, as its silhouette flared somewhat along the edges. "How should I know?"

"But do you think you could find out?" Liesl sat up on her knees and stared at Po intently. "Please? Could you just—could you just ask?"

"Maybe." Po did not want to get the girl's hopes up. The Other Side was vast and filled with ghosts. Even on the Living Side, Po could still feel the Other Side expanding in all directions, had a sense of new people crossing over endlessly into its dark and twisting corridors. And people lost shapes quickly on the Other Side, and memories, too: They became blurry, as Po had said. They became a part of darkness, of the vast spaces between stars. They became like the invisible side of the moon.

But Po knew the girl wouldn't understand any of this if it tried to explain, so it just said, "Maybe. I can try."

"Thank you!"

"I said I would try, that's all. I didn't say I could."

"Still, thank you." Liesl felt hopeful for the first time since her father had died. It had been ever so long since anyone had tried to do anything for her—not since her father had been well, at least, before Augusta had decided that Liesl must move to the attic. And that was months upon months ago: a tower of months, so that when Liesl tried to remember her life before the attic, her memory grew slimmer and slimmer as though it was being stretched, and snapped before it could reach the ground.

Po was next to her. Then it was in the corner again, a person-shaped shadow with a curious shaggy shadow-pet at its feet. Bundle did the mew-bark thing. Liesl decided it sounded like a *mwark*.

"You have to do something for me in return," Po said.

"Okay," Liesl said, feeling uneasy. She did not know what she could possibly do for a ghost, especially since she was never allowed to leave the attic. It was, Augusta said, far too dangerous; the world was a terrible place, and would eat her up. "What do you want?"

"A drawing," Po blurted, and then began to flicker again, this time from embarrassment. It was not used to having outbursts.

Liesl was relieved. "I'll draw you a train," she said passionately. She loved trains—the sound of them, at least. She heard their great horns blasting and the rattle of their wheels on the track and listened to them wailing farther and farther away, like birds calling to one another in the distance, and sometimes she confused the two sounds and imagined the train had wings that might carry its passengers up into the sky.

Po did not say anything. It seemed to pour itself into the regular corner shadows. All at once it blended in with Bundle's shadow, and then with the shadow of the crooked desk, and three-legged stool.

Liesl sighed. She was alone again.

Then Po's silhouette pulled itself abruptly away from the corner. It looked at Liesl for a moment.

"Good-bye," Po said finally. Bundle went, *Mwark*.

"Good-bye," Liesl said, but that time Po and Bundle were gone for real.

TWO

AT THE VERY MOMENT THAT LIESL WAS SPEAKING the word "Good-bye" into an empty room, a very frazzled-looking alchemist's apprentice was standing on the quiet street in front of her house, staring up at her darkened window and feeling sorry for himself.

He was wearing a large and lumpy coat that came well past his knees and had, in fact, most recently belonged to someone twice his age and size. He carried a wooden box— about the size of a loaf of bread—under one arm, and his hair was sticking up from his head at various odd angles and had in it the remnants of hay and dried leaves, because the night before he had once again messed up a potion and been forced by the alchemist to sleep out back, where the chickens and animals were.

But that wasn't why the boy, whose name was Will but who also answered to "Useless" and "Hopeless" and "Snot-Face" and "Sniveler" (at least when the alchemist was the one calling to him), felt sorry for himself.

He felt sorry for himself because for the third night in a row the pretty girl with the straight brown hair was not sitting in the small attic window, framed by the soft golden glow of the oil lamp to her left, with her eyes turned downward as though she was working on something.

"Scrat," Will said, which was what the alchemist usually said when he was upset about something. Because Will was extremely upset, he repeated it. "Scrat."

He had been sure—sure!—that she would be there tonight. That was why he had come so far out of his way; that was why he had looped all the way around to Highland Avenue instead of going directly to Ebury Street, as the alchemist had told him a dozen times he must do.

As he had walked down empty street after empty street, past row after row of darkened houses, in silence so thick it was like a syrup that dragged his footsteps away into echoes before he had placed a heel on the ground, he had imagined it perfectly: how he would come around the corner and see that tiny square of light so many stories above him, and see her face floating there like a single star. She was not, Will had decided long ago, the type of person who would call him names other than his own; she was not impatient or mean or angry or snobby.

She was perfect.

Of course, Will had never actually spoken to the girl. And some small corner of his mind told him it was stupid to continue finding excuses, every single night, to go past her window. It was a waste of time. It was, as the alchemist would have said, *useless*. (*Useless* was one of the alchemist's favorite words, and he used it interchangeably to describe Will's plans, thoughts, work, appearance, and general selfhood.)

Will was sure that if he ever had the chance to speak to the girl in the window, he would be too afraid to. Besides, he felt certain he would never have that chance. She stayed in her window, far above him; he stayed on the street, far below her. And that was how things were.

But every night for the past year since he had first seen her heart-shaped face floating there in the middle of that light, and no matter how many times he had scolded himself or tried to go in the opposite direction or sworn that he would stay away from Highland Avenue *no matter what*, his feet had seemed to circle him back toward that same stretch of sidewalk just below her window.

The truth was this: Will was lonely. During the day he studied with the alchemist, who was seventy-four years old and smelled like sour milk. At night he carried out the alchemist's errands in the darkest, loneliest, most barren corners of the city. Before discovering the girl in the window, he had sometimes gone whole weeks without seeing a single living person besides the alchemist and the strange, bent, crooked, desperate people who wheeled and dealed with him in the middle of the night. Before her, he was used to moving in darkness and silence so thick it felt like a cloak, suffocating him.

The nights were cold, and damp. He could never get the chill out of his bones, no matter how long he sat by the fire when he returned to the alchemist's house.

And then one night he had turned the corner of Highland Avenue and seen, at the very top of an enormous white house, all decorated with balconies and curlicues and designs that looked like frosting on a cake, a single warm light burning in a single tiny window like a single candle, and a girl's face in it, and the face and the light had warmed him right to the very core. Since then he had seen her every night.

But for the past three nights the window had been dark.

Will shifted the box from his left arm to his right. He had been standing on the sidewalk a long time, and the box had grown heavy. He did not know what to do. That was the problem. Above all he feared that something bad had happened to the girl, and he felt—strangely, since he had never met her or spoken a word to her in his life—that he would not forgive himself if that were the case.

He stared at the stone porch and the double doors that loomed behind the iron gate at 31 Highland Avenue. He thought about going through the gate and up the stairs and knocking with that heavy iron knocker.

"Hello," he would say. "I'm wondering about the girl in the attic."

Useless, the alchemist would say.

"Hello," he would say. "During my nightly walks I

21

could not help but notice the girl who lives upstairs. Pretty, with a heart-shaped face. I haven't seen her in several days and just wanted to see if everything is okay? You can tell her Will was asking for her."

Pathetic, the alchemist would say. *Worse than useless. As ridiculous and deluded as a frog trying to turn into a flower petal. . . .*

Just as the alchemist's remembered lecture was gaining steam in Will's overtired and indecisive mind, the miraculous happened.

The attic light went on, and against its small, soft glow Liesl's head suddenly appeared. As always, her face was tilted downward, as though she was working on something, and for a moment Will had fantasies (as he always did) that she was writing him a letter.

Dear Will, it would say. *Thank you for standing outside my window every night. Even though we've never spoken, I can't tell you how useful you have been to me. . . .*

And even though Will knew that this was absurd because (1) the girl in the window didn't know his name, and (2) she almost certainly couldn't see him standing in the pitch-black from a well-lit window, just seeing the girl and imagining the letter made him incredibly, immensely happy—so happy he didn't have a word for it, so happy it didn't feel like other kinds of happiness he knew, like getting to eat a meal when he was hungry, or (occasionally) sleep when he was very tired. It didn't even feel like watching the clouds or running as fast as he could when no one was looking. This feeling was even lighter than that, and also more satisfying somehow.

Standing on the dark street corner with the black, quiet night squeezing him like a fist from all sides, Will suddenly remembered something he had not thought of in a very long time. He remembered walking home from school to the orphanage, before he had been adopted by the alchemist, and seeing Kevin Donnell turn left in front of him and pass through a pretty painted gate.

It was snowing, and late, and already getting dark, and as Will had passed by Kevin Donnell's house, he had seen a door flung open. He had seen light and warmth and the big, comforting silhouette of a woman inside of it. He had smelled meat and soap and heard a soft trilling voice saying, *Come inside, you must be freezing.* . . . And the pain had been so sharp and deep inside of him for a second that he had looked around, thinking he must have walked straight into the point of a knife.

Looking at the girl in the attic window was like looking into Kevin Donnell's house, but without the pain.

And at that moment Will vowed that he would never let anything bad happen to the girl in the window. The idea was immediate and deadly serious; he could not let anything bad happen to her. He had some vague idea that it would be terrible for himself.

Church bells boomed out suddenly, shattering the silence, and Will jumped. Two o'clock in the morning already! He had been gone from the alchemist's for more than an hour, and he had yet to complete the tasks he had been sent out to perform.

"Go straight to the Lady Premiere," the alchemist had said, pressing the wooden box into Will's arms. "Do not stop for anyone. Hurry right there, and give this to her. Do not let anyone else see it or touch it. You are carrying great magic with you! Huge magic. The biggest I have ever made. The biggest I have ever attempted."

Will had stifled a yawn and tried to look serious. Every time the alchemist made a new potion, he said it was his greatest yet, and Will had difficulty being impressed by the words nowadays.

The alchemist, perhaps sensing this, had muttered, "Useless," under his breath. Then, frowning, he had given Will a handwritten list of items to collect from Mr. Gray, after the delivery was complete.

And now it was two o'clock, and Will had neither seen the Lady Premiere nor visited Mr. Gray at his work space.

Will made a sudden decision. The Lady Premiere lived all the way on the other side of the city, near the alchemist's shop, while the gray man was no more than a few blocks away from where he was standing. If he delivered the magic first, he would have to cross the whole city, then cross back, then cross back again, and he would not be home in time to sleep more than an hour. Really, he should not have come to see the girl in the window; it was absurd. But he could not feel even a little bit bad about it. In fact he felt better than he had in days.

No. He would go to Mr. Gray first and then deliver the magic to the Lady on his way back to the shop, and the alchemist would never know the difference. Besides—Will shifted the box again—the potion was no doubt an every-day kind of magic dust, for curing warts or growing hair or keeping memories longer or something like that.

Will dug into his pocket and pulled out the crumpled list the alchemist had scrawled hastily on a scrap of paper. Nothing too unusual: a dead man's beard, some fingernail clippings, two chicken heads, the eye of a blind frog.

Yes, Will decided, casting one last look at the girl in the window before setting off. Groceries first; and after that, the magic.

Up in her room, Liesl drew a train with wings, floating through the sky.

THREE

AT THE END OF A TINY, WINDY STREET AND DOWN
a steep flight of narrow wooden stairs and past a sign
that said

THE ATELIER OF GRAY.

BODY DISPOSAL, CORPSES,

ANIMAL AND HUMAN PARTS

(SINCE 1885),

Mr. Gray was feeling very annoyed.

For the fourth time in two weeks, Mr. Gray was completely and entirely out of urns.

The problem was how rapidly people were dying. If they
would just stop dying, stop even for a week to give his urn
maker and his casket maker time to catch up . . .

He stroked his chin thoughtfully. Perhaps he could request that the mayor order that there be no deaths for a week? Or impose a death tax? He shook his head. No, no, impossible.

He knew enough about death to know that it could not be bribed, bought, delayed, or put off. He had lived in the cold basement rooms beneath the funeral home of his great-great-great-grandfather for his whole life. As a child he had played with the loosened gold teeth of the dead men, spinning them across the floor like tops and watching them catch the light. He had been a gravestone maker and a gravedigger, an executioner for the state, a mercy killer, a mummifier.

These days he mostly stuck to the simple stuff: burning and burying. When someone died, he either put the body in a nice wood coffin lined with sober black silk, or he put the body headfirst in the oven and, when it had burned away to ashes, placed these in a nice decorative urn, which could be kept neatly on display on a mantel or a shelf or a bedside table. Mr. Gray's great-uncle, for example, was kept within Urn Style #27 (Grecian) just above the stove in the kitchen; his mother was in Urn Style #4 (Lavish) on the windowsill overlooking the street, and his father, in Urn Style #12 (Sober), was sitting next to her. Mr. Gray liked to have his family all around him.

Of course, he still did a little bit of dealing on the side—odds and ends, bits and pieces, toes and fingernails, animal blood, this and that. These were the scraps that a nighttime business, a business of death, was built on, and Mr. Gray was only happy to pass along the dried and dead and shriveled things, the squirmy and wormy things, the rot, that came his way.

He shook his head and began rummaging under the kitchen sink for an empty container to hold the mortal remains of a certain John C. Smith, bar owner, who had arrived at his door that morning.

Only three days ago he had been forced to sacrifice his mother's old wooden jewelry box in the service of his profession. It was sitting on the kitchen table now, full of ash. He had regretted using the jewelry box for such a purpose, but he could not very well send the widowed Mrs. Morbower home with a cereal box containing her dead husband, as he had done earlier in the week with Mrs. Kittle. . . . Not after Mrs. Morbower had paid him so well and so quickly to have the body burned to ash. . . .

Mr. Gray sighed. If people would only stop dying. Just for a week! He was sure a week was all he needed. . . .

Tap-tap-tap.

A soft knocking shook Mr. Gray from his reverie. He went

to the door of his atelier and looked through the grimy window to the narrow street. He saw nothing but a patch of black hair sprouting at the very bottom of the window. The alchemist's boy: Billy or Michael or something-or-other, Mr. Gray could never remember. All children were the same to him: strange and sticky and best avoided, like an upright variety of jellyfish.

But he opened the door.

"Hello," Will said nervously, as Mr. Gray loomed before him. He shifted the box of magic in his arms—his left arm had started to cramp, from holding the wooden box for so long—and handed Mr. Gray the list the alchemist had written for him. "Here for a pickup, please."

Mr. Gray's long, thin face grew even longer and thinner as he scanned the list. "Come in," he said finally, and stepped backward so Will could pass through the door.

The smell hit Will as soon as he entered the small front room that served as Mr. Gray's kitchen, work space, and receiving room. No matter how many times he came for a pickup, Will could never get used to it: a bitter, scorching smell mixed with the smell of bodies, like a fire lit in the very center of a dirty stable. He pretended to scratch his nose, and he breathed into the fabric of his coat sleeve.

Mr. Gray didn't seem to notice. He was still reviewing

the alchemist's list, muttering things like, "Yes, fine, okay" or "Well, I'm not sure about two chicken heads" or "A dead man's beard? I might have a mustache somewhere."

Finally Mr. Gray looked up, stroking his chin. "You may as well sit," he said. "This might take a little while."

"Thank you." Will did not really want to sit at Mr. Gray's table, which was cluttered with mysterious jars of things and various foul-smelling chemicals, but he did as he was told because he had always been slightly afraid of Mr. Gray and did not want to anger him. He placed the wooden box of magic on the table, next to another wooden box that looked relatively plain but probably (Will knew) contained chicken hearts or something equally nasty, and sat down. It was, at least, a relief to be off his feet.

Mr. Gray disappeared into one of his other rooms, and Will heard the sounds of rattling and banging and soft exclamations of "Now where was . . . ?" and "I could have sworn I had . . ." Will did his best not to look around too much. On one of his first visits to Mr. Gray he had made the mistake of approaching a large glass jar, like the kind you store pickles in, and had found it to be full of eyeballs. Since then he was careful to avoid exploring Mr. Gray's rooms. Instead he kept his eyes fixed on the flames dancing in the enormous furnace in the corner, which sent strange shadows skating and leaping over the walls.

Will knew that the furnace was used for burning bodies, but still, he found it kind of pretty . . . ribbons of blue and red and white, twisting beyond the grate . . . colors you never saw anymore. . . . His eyes became heavy and his head began to nod forward on his neck. It had been a long night.

Then Will was climbing up a long silk braid of hair, woven with multicolored strands. He was climbing into the sky, where a steam-engine train was waiting, engine chugging, puffing out smoke that blended with the clouds. Strangely, the train had wings—great big feathery wings, like the wings of an enormous bird. The train was painted in bright colors, many of which Will did not have a name for; and in one of the windows he saw the girl from 31 Highland Avenue, looking out at him and waving. She was saying something to him—she was calling his name? No. She was telling him her name . . . Amanda . . . or Amen . . . or . . .

"Ahem."

Will woke with a start and found Mr. Gray looking at him, holding a small canvas sack from which various paper-wrapped objects were protruding.

"Here." Mr. Gray extended the sack to Will. "I did the

best I could. Tell Merv"——that was the alchemist's name, which no one but Mr. Gray ever used——"that I had absolutely no chicken heads to give him. Mrs. Finnegan came by yesterday and cleaned me out entirely. She was making soup."

"Mmmkay." Will got clumsily to his feet. His body felt heavy all over, and he was groggy from sleep and the sudden, rude awakening from his dream. He took the bag from Mr. Gray and slung it over one shoulder. From its depths came the smell of dried fish and other sour things. He took the wooden box from the table. It felt even heavier than it had earlier in the night. "Thank you."

"Until next time," Mr. Gray said, and was relieved when the boy tottered out of the door with his bag and his box. Really, just like a jellyfish, he thought disapprovingly; all pale and wiggly-looking, like he could squirm away from you quickly. Children in general, Mr. Gray thought, were incredibly inconvenient. Someday he hoped the world could be rid of them altogether. Perhaps he could ask the mayor . . . ?

Another shake of his head, and a sigh. No, no. It wouldn't do. That was life: You were born, you were a child, then you grew and you died. Even Mr. Gray had been a child once, though he hardly remembered it——and even then he had always worn the same somber black suits, and neckties every day. Even his first-grade teacher had called him Mr. Gray.

The alchemist's assistant's visit had distracted him, and for a moment he stood in the middle of the room, trying to recall what he had been doing before the interruption. Oh, yes! Looking for a suitable container for Mr. Smith's remains. He went back to rummaging under the sink and eventually came out with an empty canister of coffee.

It was all very strange, Mr. Gray thought, as he wiped the coffee canister clean with a sponge. Very, very mysterious. You were born; you lived a whole life; and at the end, you wound up in a coffee container.

"Ah, well," he said out loud quietly. "That's just the way things are. Life's a funny business." Death, he supposed, was the punch line.

On the cramped wooden table the very powerful magic sitting in a small wooden chest that looked almost exactly like the late Mrs. Gray's jewelry box let off a sparkle, a minute flash of light. But Mr. Gray had his back toward the table and did not see.

And outside, in the dark maze of sleeping streets, the alchemist's assistant scuttled off toward the Lady Premiere carrying a wooden jewelry box filled with the mortal remains of Liesl Morbower's father.

Coincidences; mix-ups; harmless mistakes and switches. And so a story is born.

What Mr. Gray had said was true: Life is a very funny business indeed.

FOUR

THE NIGHT AFTER LIESL FIRST SAW THE GHOST and the ghost-pet, they appeared again. But this time she was waiting for them.

"Did you find out? Did you see him? Is he on the Other Side?" she asked breathlessly, as soon as she saw Po flickering in the corner of the room.

"Turn off the light, please," Po said. Po liked the light—it craved the light, to be honest, since the Other Side was in darkness all the time—but it was no longer used to it. And it was one thing to see the bright glow of the lamp from the Other Side. By the time it reached Po there, it had been filtered through layers and layers of existence, like sunlight getting bent and pale through water.

It was quite another thing to step into the Living Side, and see the light full-on, with its blare and glare.

Po did not really have eyes anymore, nor did it really have a head to host a headache; but standing in the light made something tremble and ache inside of it.

Liesl was impatient to hear news of her father, but she stood up and moved to the lamp and extinguished it. Strangely, she could see Po and Bundle better in the dark. Their forms seemed clearer and more solid. In the light they had looked like skating shadows at the edges of her vision; when she tried to focus on them, they dissolved.

"Well?" Liesl demanded. Her hands were shaking, and she heard her heart go *womp-womp-womp* painfully in her chest as she waited for the ghost's answer.

"You didn't say hello," Po said.

"What?"

"You said that people on the Living Side always say hello to each other," Po said, and Liesl could tell from the way it faded that it had been offended. "But you didn't say it."

"I forgot," Liesl said sharply. She would have strangled the ghost, if it had had a head or neck or body. "We had a deal, remember? You promised you would look for my father."

"I remember," Po said, and didn't say anything more.

Liesl took a deep breath. She realized if she lost her temper, the ghost might simply go away. She tried to start again, from the beginning. "Hello," she said.

"Hello," Po said.

"How are you?"

"Tired," Po said. It had been across incredible distances; it had covered vast, unimaginable tracts of time since it had last spoken with Liesl the night before. It had been across eons that stretched like deserts across the universe: places where time was as water in the Sahara—gone, drifting to dust. It had been into cold, black seas where souls huddled together, and into dark tunnels burned straight into the center of existence, which led forever away, away, away.

But it could tell none of this to Liesl, so it just repeated, "Very, very tired."

"Oh?" Liesl dug her fingernails into her palms. She was itching to ask about her father again, but she forced herself to remember her manners. "Did you have a long day?"

For a second she swore the ghost laughed. Then she thought the wind had only blown in through the attic window for a second, rustling the papers on her desk. "Longer than long. It took forever."

Liesl did not know that Po meant this literally, and thought it was a stupid thing to say. But she stopped herself from saying so. "I'm very sorry to hear you are tired," she said stiffly, her inside voice screaming: *Tell me what you know about my dad! Tell me now or I'll kill you again! I'll make you a double-ghost!*

"What does that mean? What does it mean to say you're sorry?"

Liesl groped for words to describe it. "It means—it means what it means. It means that I feel bad. It means that I wish I could make you untired."

Po flipped upside down and then righted itself, still obviously confused. "But why should you wish anything for me?"

"It's an expression," Liesl said. Then she thought hard for a minute. "People need other people to feel things for them," she said. "It gets lonely to feel things all by yourself."

Po appeared next to her. And suddenly she felt Bundle around her, a pile in her lap, a bare outline in the dark. The ghost-pet had no warmth or weight, but still she could *sense* it. It was hard to describe: as though the darkness beside her had texture, suddenly, like a deep drift of velvet.

Po asked, "Did you remember the drawing?"

Liesl had drawn Po a train with wings attached to its side: great big feathery wings, like those of the sparrows she saw perched on the rooftops directly across from her window. She passed the drawing to the ghost before remembering that the ghost had no hands with which to grab the sheet of paper. Instead she held it out, and the ghost looked at it thoughtfully for a minute or two.

At last the ghost seemed satisfied and said, "I've found your father for you. He is on the Other Side." Bundle made a mewing noise in the back of its throat.

Liesl did not know whether to be relieved or unhappy, so she felt both at the same time: a terrible feeling, like two sharp blades running through her in different directions. "Are you—are you sure? Is it definitely him?"

"I'm sure," Po said, and stood again, drifting like a mist to the middle of the room.

"Did you—did you speak to him? Did you speak to him about me?" Liesl's voice was a bare squeak. "Did you tell him I miss him? And did you tell him good-bye?"

"There was no time," Po said, and Liesl thought she heard something in its voice. A sadness, perhaps.

Po *was* sad, because the ghost knew that in the vast oceans of time that surrounded it endlessly on either side, somehow there was never enough time for the very things you needed to say and do. But it would not tell Liesl that.

Liesl's eyes were bright. Even when she was sad, she seemed full of hope. You could see the hope shining off her: It made its own glow, as though inside of her a lamp was illuminated.

Liesl was silent for a minute. "What does it mean?" she said finally. "That he is there, on the Other Side? I mean, why hasn't he . . . gone Beyond?"

Po shrugged. "It depends. It could mean lots of things. He is still—*attached* to the Living Side. Waiting for something, maybe."

"Waiting for *what*?" Liesl could hardly stand it. She couldn't stand not to know; she couldn't stand not to be able to speak to him, and ask. The heaviness pressed down on her chest, and she felt like curling up in a ball, and closing her eyes, and sleeping. But Po was there, watching her, and Bundle was still a soft fold of darkness in her lap, so she didn't.

Po thought about the man who had shuffled by him in the endless line of new souls, shaking his head, with his hair sticking up every which way as though he had just been rudely and suddenly awakened from a nap. He had been speaking to a soul coming along directly behind him, repeating the same story over and over. That was a thing about the recently dead. They still spoke to one another out loud. They had not yet learned to communicate without words. They had not learned the language of the deepest pools of the universe; the high, unvoiced rhythms of the planets in orbit; the language of being and breath.

"He spoke of a willow tree," Po said. "The willow tree stood next to a lake, and he spoke of wanting to go there again."

Liesl's heart tightened in her chest. For a moment she couldn't say anything at all. Then she burst out, "So you aren't lying. You did see him after all."

"Of course I'm not lying." Po's edges flared. "Ghosts never lie. We have no reason to."

Liesl did not notice that Po had been offended. "I remember the willow tree, and the lake. That's where my mother was buried. We used to go there, before—before—" At the last second Liesl couldn't say *before my dad met Augusta* or *before we moved to Dirge* or *before he got sick* or *before Augusta locked me in the attic*. She had almost forgotten there *was* a Before.

Now she remembered. And so she squeezed her eyes

tight and climbed down the tower of months she had been in the attic, reaching back and back into the rooms of her memory that were dusty and so dim she could catch only little, flickering glances of things. There! Her father leading her into the shade of the great willow tree, patterns of green dancing across his cheeks. And there! Liesl laying her cheek on the velvety soft moss that grew above her mother's grave. And there! If she turned to the left—if she concentrated hard enough—flaring to life in front of her: her father's kind blue eyes, the comforting roughness of his arms around her, his voice in her ear saying, "Someday I'll come back here, to lie beside your mother again."

"The sun still shined then," Liesl said. It had been a long time since she had said the word *sun*. It had a strange, light taste in her mouth.

Liesl had long ago lost count, but the sun had not come out in 1,728 days. One day the clouds had come, as they often had before. Nobody was especially concerned. The clouds would surely break up tomorrow, or the next day, or certainly the day after that.

But they had not broken up for 1,728 days in a row. Sometimes it rained. In the winter there was hail and slush. But it was never sunny.

Over time, the grass had withered into dirt. Flowers had curled back deep on themselves, withdrawing into the ground, seeds that could never bloom. The whole world was a dull gray color, even the people in it—everything the bland pale gray of vegetables that had been boiled into slime. Only potatoes grew with any regularity; and all across the world, people starved.

Even those who ate well—the rich—were starving, though they could not have said for what, exactly. But they woke with a gnawing hunger in their stomachs and chests, hunger so fierce and overwhelming it crippled them, made them bend over with sudden cries of pain, made them almost nauseous.

"It was a long time ago," Po said.

"Longer." Liesl felt heavy again. She repeated the word *ineffable* clearly, three times, in her head, lingering over the gentle slope of the double *f*s, like the soft peaks of the whipped cream she remembered from her early childhood, and this made her feel slightly better.

"They brought him here today, you know. I heard the servants talking. Through the radiator." Liesl pointed to the radiator in the corner. Sometimes, when she got very lonely, she lay down there and pressed her ear to the floor, where a small hole allowed a water pipe to pass through between floors. Through it she could often hear two of her stepmother's servants, Tessie and Karen, conversing in their bedroom below. "They took his body and they turned it into ash, and they put the ash in a wooden box, and Karen got it today from Mr. Gray. They will bury the box in the backyard." For a moment she was overcome. She closed her eyes, and when she opened them, she saw two disks of moonlight staring unblinkingly back at her. Bundle was still in her lap, watching her.

"If you see him again, will you give him a message for me?" Liesl asked Po.

"The chances I will see him again are next to nothing," Po said. The ghost did not want the girl to get her hopes up. It might not even recognize Liesl's father if it saw him again; by then, Liesl's father might not recognize himself. He might have begun to blur, letting the infinity tug on him gently from all sides, like sand being pulled by an eternal tide. He might have already begun the process of becoming part of the Everything. He would begin to feel the electricity from distant stars pulsing through him like a heartbeat. He would feel the weight of old planets on his shoulders, and he would feel the winds of distant corners of the universe blowing through him.

"*Next* to nothing," Liesl retorted, "but not nothing."

Liesl was quite right about this. Nothing in the world is ever really nothing, and everything is possible in some way, and Po knew it. The ghost made a full turn in the air, which Liesl (correctly) assumed meant that the ghost had taken her point.

"Tell him," Liesl said, and found that she was choking up and couldn't speak. There was so much she wanted to say and so much she wanted to ask, but she refused to cry in front of anyone, especially a ghostly someone, and so she just said, "Tell him I miss him." Then she turned her face into the sleeve of her nightshirt.

"All right," Po said. "If you'll make another drawing for me."

Liesl nodded.

"Good-bye," Po said. Bundle vanished from her lap. The darkness there suddenly became empty.

"Wait!" Liesl called the ghosts back. She was desperate not to be alone again. "Did my father say anything else? Anything at all?"

Her face was turned up toward Po, and all that hope was clearly there, shining, as bright as the sun that had shone long ago.

"He said that he missed you," Po said. "He said good-bye."

Liesl made a little cry: a sound that was both happy and sad, Po thought, although it couldn't be sure.

It did not stay to find out. Po had already been too long on the Living Side for one night, and the ghost let itself sink back into the softness and the deepness of the Other Side with something like relief.

Two visits to the Living Side, and the ghost had already become a little more human.

Po had remembered how to lie.

FIVE

THAT VERY SAME NIGHT, THE ALCHEMIST'S
apprentice was once again weaving his way through the
dark and silent city streets, this time struggling to keep
up with his master. He pulled his oversized coat closer and
ducked his head against the wind, which was fierce and
deathly cold. Winter had arrived, there was no doubt about
it. The air was full of a wet, sleeting rain, and it stung Will's
cheeks like shards of cut glass.

The alchemist whipped around and urged him on.
"Faster," he barked. There was a bit of moisture hanging
from the tip of his nose, and it trembled a bit before receding into his left nostril. "The Lady Premiere won't like to be
kept waiting."

Will tried to urge his feet to move faster, but they seemed

to be encased in solid blocks of ice. It was not just the cold, either. His whole body felt heavy, from the top of his head to the tips of his toes. Even his hair felt weightier than usual.

The problem was simple: He was exhausted. By the time he had returned from making his delivery to the Lady Premiere the night before, it was close to four o'clock in the morning. The alchemist had awakened him at six thirty with a swift kick to the ribs. Will had accidentally overslept his alarm; he was supposed to be out at six to feed the enormous, slimy, bleary-eyed catfish that lived in the foul-smelling pool of water behind the alchemist's living quarters. Then he had spent the whole day grinding up cow eyes, and measuring the blood of lizards into different-sized vials, and mixing and labeling, while the alchemist watched and criticized. Nothing Will ever did seemed to be correct: The word *useless* had been thrown around a record sixty-seven times just between the hours of four and six p.m.

And then, just as Will was sinking into his small cot at eleven thirty p.m.—for once, with no deliveries and no pickups to make—a messenger had rapped sharply at the door. The alchemist was requested at the house of the Lady Premiere, on a matter of some urgency.

"This is it," the alchemist had said, his voice trembling

with emotion, after the messenger had departed. "This is the moment I've been waiting for my whole life. She is going to make me Official. You just wait and see. It is because of the magic I made for her." Then he glanced sharply in Will's direction. "And you *will* see. You must come with me, and take notes. That way, when I'm Official, and my talent is recognized far and wide, there will be a record of the moment of my ascension."

And so here Will was, trekking through the dark and ice-covered streets at midnight, returning to the Lady Premiere's estate for the second time in twenty-four hours.

"Faster!" bellowed the alchemist, without bothering to turn around this time. "What's wrong with you? Have you forgotten how to walk? Useless!"

The alchemist's boots rang out sharply on the pavement, so that more than one child—sleeping in the darkened rooms above the street—had their dreams punctuated by the sound of ice picks, or knives clashing with other knives, or hammers coming down on glass.

The alchemist could hardly contain his excitement. If it had been up to him, he would have sprouted a pair of wings and flown to the Lady Premiere. But that was impractical, of course. Falcons' talons were almost impossible to find nowadays, and the cheaper pigeons' talons were almost useless for growing wings: The one time he had made a potion from them, his client had reported no more than a pair of long, limp feathers that sprouted halfheartedly from his shoulder blades.

So they walked. Or rather, the alchemist walked. The boy

seemed to drag, inch, *ooze* along like a gigantic slug. For the eighty millionth time, the alchemist wished that when he had gone to the orphanage to select an apprentice, he had selected someone—anyone!—else. Even the girl who was missing both arms would have been preferable.

"Faster!" he screeched again.

It was only the second time the alchemist had left his little ramshackle apartment in more than a decade. The first time he had been forced to go select a new apprentice from the orphanage, after the last one had had an unfortunate accident with a transfiguration potion and had been turned into a mouse—just as the alchemist's scrawny, always hungry tabby cat had come swishing in through the cat door. That apprentice had been hopeless too: really, an absolute pig. Even his death had been messy—little mouse parts scattered everywhere. The alchemist shuddered to think about it.

In general, the alchemist saw no reason to venture beyond the comfortable limits of his home and studio. Work was everything to him, and he had his apprentice to run the errands necessary for the job. The alchemist was a scientist, not a foot messenger, always darting to and fro. He preferred to spend his time on his trials and experiments, tinkering with the old recipes, trying out new ones—all in search of ever greater, deeper, bigger magic.

Besides, the alchemist despised people. He tried to avoid interacting with them whenever he could. They did not respect him. They did not respect his science. They referred to him as a hack or, even worse, as a magician.

Even thinking the word made the alchemist choke a little reflexively. A magician! Ha. Clowns—that's what they were. Illusionists, smoke and mirrors, card tricks and birthday parties.

The alchemist was the real deal. He worked in potions and transfigurations. He turned frogs into goats and goats into mugs of tea. He made people grow wings or third legs. Recently he had mastered a tincture that would make a person disappear entirely.

His was an ancient art, one that had been passed from generation to generation, in whispered secrets and dusty volumes and jotted notes, now nearly faded to illegibility, scrawled on sheets of vellum.

Long ago, when he had still gone out into the world more frequently, he had shivered and shriveled inside whenever he heard the word *magician* shouted at him from the open windows, whenever he looked up and saw children pointing to him with expressions of delight, calling, "Do a card trick! Do the one with the ace that disappears!" As though he was no better than a trained performing monkey.

Well. All that would soon change.

The alchemist knew that the potion he had mixed for the Lady Premiere was something special. It was undoubtedly his most powerful magic yet. He had been perfecting that particular brand of magic for years, ever since he had come across the promise of its results, written in the margin of an ancient volume of spells and potions.

The little poem was only three lines long, but the words seemed to carry the power of their promise. They pulsed with energy. The alchemist remembered how the poem had even appeared to glow slightly on the page.

The dead will rise

From glade to glen

And ancient will be young again.

Below these lines an additional note had been written:

The Most Powerful Magic in the World (use sparingly).

The meaning was clear enough. The magic could restore youth to the old and bring the dead back to life: ancient, dangerous, powerful magic.

It had been a complicated and difficult magic to make and control. Just the ingredients required had, at first, been enough to discourage him. A perfect snowflake! The laughter of a child! A summer afternoon! The alchemist had never seen a spell quite like it.

And then, of course, there was the most difficult ingredient of all to procure: *pure sunlight (1 cup)*.

That had been tricky. Very tricky and troublesome indeed. He had nearly given up on several occasions; it was very hard to bottle pure sunlight, and over the years the alchemist had had to suck and bleed and wheedle the sky dry, until the sun shriveled up entirely and the world turned to gray.

But he had done it. After five long years, the alchemist had done it.

And now the Lady Premiere would acknowledge his genius and celebrate his masterpiece, and he would become the Official Alchemist of the State, or the First Alchemist of the Highest Order, and he would attend state dinners and distribute thick cream-colored business cards with his name and title printed neatly on them—but not his number. It would be for him to decide whom he wanted to contact, and when. And he would have a real laboratory for his experiments, and absolutely no one would dare call him Magician anymore.

At last they had reached the tall wrought-iron fence that encircled the Lady Premiere's six-story town house. Beyond the gates a rising mist made it impossible to see the Lady Premiere's vast residence clearly. But various lit windows smoldered there beyond the fog, and made the alchemist think of rich upholstered furniture, and gold, and dark wood. He was very eager to get inside. The Lady Premiere was a princess in her native country—was it Austria or Russia? The alchemist could never remember. No, no. Perhaps it was Germany. Difficult to know. He had heard different things at different times. In any case, she was wonderfully and fabulously wealthy, and as a favorite of the mayor's, she was also extremely powerful.

At the gates a guard halted their progress. The alchemist could barely announce himself, he was so excited.

"And who's that?" the guard asked, nodding toward Will.

"Nobody," the alchemist said. "He's just my apprentice." He was annoyed that the guard had reminded him of the boy's existence—he had almost managed to forget him entirely. It was necessary that someone be there to witness and record his meeting with the Lady Premiere, but the alchemist wished it could have been otherwise.

There was a curious, rattling sound coming from the boy now. The alchemist frowned. The boy's teeth were chattering—that was it—bouncing off each other with a noise like a bunch of dice rolling around in a wooden box. The alchemist squeezed his fists together and breathed heavily through his nose, trying to stay calm. When he became Official, he would get a real assistant, not some scrimp of a shrimp of a boy who couldn't even keep his teeth from knocking together in public.

"It's awfully late for the boy to be out," the guard said thoughtfully. The alchemist could tell he was slow.

"He's fine," the alchemist snapped.

"He looks cold." The guard now sounded reproachful. "He should have a hat, at least. His ears is as purple as a rib steak."

"He's no concern of yours." The alchemist was losing his temper. "Your *concern* is to announce us, and escort us inside. We are expected, and we are already late, and I doubt you can afford to upset the Lady Premiere."

The guard shot one more look at Will, who was trying very hard to keep his teeth from bouncing together, having stuffed a corner of his coat sleeve in his mouth, and then stepped back inside the small stone guard hut. He began cranking a lever; slowly, the iron gates groaned open.

"Go on, then," the guard called out to them, and the alchemist and his apprentice passed into the mist-enshrouded courtyard.

SIX

THE GUARD'S NAME WAS MO, SHORT FOR MOLASSES, as in *slow as molasses* or *thick as molasses*. The nickname had been his since he was so young he no longer remembered what his real name was. And it was true that from his earliest infancy, although his heart was as big and as warm and as generous as an open hand, his brain had seemed just a tiny bit small.

Once Mo had closed the gates, he returned to his little stone hut, and his half-eaten sandwich of butter and canned sardines, and his mug of thick hot chocolate, which every night he poured carefully into a thermos labeled COFFEE. The other guards had made fun of him for preferring hot chocolate to coffee, and called him a wimp and a child, and so this was his solution: He had become a secret sipper.

There was a slapping sound, and then a low mewling in the corner. Lefty, Mo's black-and-white-striped tabby cat, had just come swinging through the large cat door Mo had fitted carefully into the back wall of the guard hut, so the cat could go directly out into an alley where she could play and sniff and roam at will.

"Hiya, Lefty," Mo cooed. Two fluorescent green eyes blinked back at him. He removed a sardine from his sandwich and held it out to her. Lefty materialized from the shadows and took the sardine from Mo's hand, afterward licking each of Mo's fingers with a rough pink tongue. "Thatta girl," Mo said fondly.

Lefty mewled again, then turned and shot once more out the cat door, which banged and shuddered in the cat's wake.

When Mo was finished with his sandwich and had taken a last, satisfied slurp of his hot chocolate, he settled his hat more firmly over his ears, slumped down a bit in his chair, and promptly fell asleep. He dreamed of many strange things—at one point he was standing at the fishmonger, but the fishmonger was a sardine, and refusing to wait on him—and then, as so often happened, he dreamed of his sister.

In his dream she was wearing her pink-and-blue-striped pajamas, as she had been the last time he had seen her. She had her favorite stuffed animal in her lap: a ratty lamb with one eye missing and stuffing coming out of its socket.

She was cross-legged on the floor of his bedroom, except the bedroom was not the bedroom of his childhood but his bedroom now, with its bare stone floor (he had had to take up the carpet, after the fleas) and its plain whitewashed walls and its single mattress, as hard as a chair.

"Hi," she said to Mo quite casually, as though she had not been missing for nearly twenty years, and as always in his dreams, Mo was at first too overwhelmed to speak. His gigantic heart seemed to be having some sort of convulsion. He was flooded with emotions, all tugging at him from different sides, like wrestlers grappling somewhere deep inside his chest. Relief that she was alive; joy at finding her again; anger that she had stayed away so long; despair that he was so much older now, and she was still so young, and they had missed so much time together.

"Where have you been all this time?" he managed finally. "We searched everywhere for you."

"Under the bed," his sister said. She had a nickname just like he did, except that hers, Bella, meant *beautiful*, and she had earned it by being the most beautiful child in a three-mile radius, and possibly everywhere.

"Under the bed?" Mo felt tremendously confused. A small corner of his brain said, *That's impossible* and *You must be dreaming*, but he swatted that part away like a fly. He did not want Bella to be a dream. He wanted her to be real. "All this time? How did you eat?"

"Lefty brought me food," Bella said, laughing, as though it was obvious, and just then Mo's cat streaked by, a blur of fur.

"Look, I'll show you." She tugged his hand and made him kneel down and peer under the bed. He felt awkward— he was so much bigger than her now! They had been almost exactly the same size before she had disappeared. He felt he must seem like a clumsy giant to her.

"Come on." Bella scampered into the space under the bed, then turned around and held out a hand. "There's plenty of room."

"I'll never fit," Mo said shyly. Bella's eyes winked out at him from the dark space under the bed. "You were really here all this time?"

At that moment, Mo began to hear muffled shouts from below. His parents. His mother and father were calling them down to dinner.

"It wasn't that bad." Bella shrugged. "The only problem

was how cold it got." The shouting grew louder, more insistent. They must hurry. His mother hated it when they were late to dinner.

"You were cold?" Mo asked.

"So cold," Bella said, and now her breath came out in little clouds, and Mo could see she was shivering. It was cold under the bed, he realized: It was absolutely freezing. Bella's teeth were clattering together.

The voices from below, sharper, sounding angry: "Where are you? Where have you gone? We need you for dinner!"

"You should have a hat, Bella-Bee," Mo said, and just then he woke up, and found himself staring not at the darkness under the bed of his dream, but into the darkness of the space under his desk, and into the pale and terrified face of the hatless boy from earlier that night. His teeth were clattering together, just as Bella's had been in the dream.

Still groggy from his nap, Mo could not even be surprised. "Why, hello," he said, rubbing his eyes and yawning. "What on earth are you—"

The boy made a frantic *no-no-no* gesture with his head and then lifted his fingers to his lips. At that moment

Mo realized that the shouting he had heard in his dreams was, in fact, real shouting from outside.

From the courtyard he heard a man calling out, "Where are you, you useless, worthless shrivel-head? When I find you, I swear, I'll cook you for dinner and turn your innards to meat loaf!" He recognized the man's voice: It was the one with the dripping nose, the man who had introduced himself as the alchemist.

Hmph, thought Mo. Not nearly so nice as being called down for dinner—being turned *into* dinner.

"He won't come out if you threaten him," he heard the Lady Premiere say sharply. Then her voice, crooning softly, "Come on, dear. It's all right. Everybody makes mistakes. Just come on out and tell us where the real magic is, and we'll give you a nice present. Maybe something hot to drink, or a new pair of mittens."

There was something very disturbing about hearing the Lady Premiere's voice so soft and slippery sounding. It was off, somehow, like seeing a bunch of roses laid over a rotting corpse.

"I'll give him a poker in his stomach," the alchemist ranted. "I'll give him slugs in his eye sockets!"

"Would you shut up!" the Lady Premiere snapped.

Mo swung his legs off the desk and stood up, smashing his hat down on his forehead.

"You see?" he whispered to the boy, pointing to his head. "You need one of these. Would keep you nice and toasty, that's for sure. Heat goes right out your head, see, if you don't have a hat to keep it all swirly and whirly warm."

The boy pointed toward the courtyard, then pointed to himself, then made another frantic *no-no-no* gesture.

"Don't worry," Mo said, winking. "Your secret's safe with me." He made a little X over his chest, directly above the place where his enormous heart was thumping, and clomped out into the courtyard to see what all the fuss was about.

The Lady Premiere and the alchemist were standing in the middle of the swirling mist. Mo felt a little colder as he approached the Lady Premiere. It was no wonder she wore those enormous fur coats with all the animal tails, Mo thought, coats that reached from the nape of her neck to the cobblestones. Privately he suspected she had ice running through her veins instead of blood.

But he forced himself to say cheerfully, "Evening, boss. Can I help you with something?"

The Lady Premiere turned her large violet eyes on him:

eyes that were rumored to be the most beautiful in all the city. "We are looking for a boy," she said coldly. "Have you seen one?"

"A boy?" Mo repeated. He dug a nail under the band of his hat and scratched his head. It was at times like these that the reputation for being an idiot was quite useful.

"Yes, a boy," the alchemist exploded. "The boy who was with me earlier. The useless, treacherous, evil . . ." Then he trailed off and began to moan. "He's trying to ruin me. That's what he wants. He wants to keep me unofficial forever. After all I've done for him . . . raised him like my own son . . ."

"Stop your moaning," the Lady Premiere said sharply. "I can't stand it. Besides, perhaps it's true what the boy said. Perhaps there really was a mix-up. We must go to Mr. Gray at once and retrieve the magic."

"There was no mix-up," the alchemist muttered darkly. "He stole the magic and intends to pass it off as his own. He means to ruin me. After all I've done! When I find him, I'll skin him from the toes up! No—from the ears down! No, from the fingers—"

"Enough!" the Lady Premiere thundered. Her voice sounded through the courtyard, loud as a rifle shot. Even Mo jumped a little.

The Lady Premiere took a deep breath, closed her eyes, and counted to three. As always, when she felt her anger bubbling and rising inside of her like a hot, dark dust, the smell of cabbage and damp socks seemed to rise up too. It was the terrible, choking smell of the house in Howard's Glen, floating out of the past to torture her. . . .

She pushed the thought quickly out of her mind. Those days were over, dead, buried. She had made sure of that. Instead she imagined her closets lined in deep purple velvet, and all the beautiful jewels glittering on her shelves, and the ninety-two pairs of shoes she had lined up neatly on beautiful oak shoe racks, and it calmed her down somewhat. Her things—her rooms—the whisper of silk sheets and the murmurings of an attentive staff—protected her from the trials and idiocies of the outside world.

"Do you have the counterfeit box?" the Lady Premiere asked more calmly, opening her eyes.

The alchemist nodded.

"Give it here."

He hesitated for only a second, then passed over Mr. Gray's mother's wooden jewelry box, which Will had accidentally taken from the table.

The Lady Premiere said to Mo, "Guard, open the gate."

Mo moved obediently to the hand crank and began slowly winding open the gate. The Lady Premiere strode quickly toward the street, then paused, turning back to the alchemist, who was still shaking his head and muttering something about "unofficial" and "ruined."

"Well?" she said. "Come along."

"Me? You want me to go *with* you?" The alchemist forced a laugh. He would never admit it, but he had always been a little bit afraid of the tall, thin, somber Mr. Gray, who kept company with the dead and knew all their secrets. "But I couldn't possibly—at this late hour—quite out of the question—the demands of my profession—"

The Lady Premiere fixed him with such an evil stare that he stopped short and shrank further into his large coat. She returned to the courtyard, walking so slowly and deliberately she reminded Mo of an enormous cat.

"Perhaps you don't understand," she said softly, and Mo shivered. The gentleness in her voice was the most terrifying of all. "I am the Lady Premiere in this city, and I asked you to deliver me the most powerful magic in the world. Instead you deliver me this—this—this—" She held up the wooden jewelry box and whipped open its lid. A little bit of gray ash floated off in the wind. "This *dirt*. This *worthlessness*." She snapped the lid closed again, so close to the alchemist's nose that he flinched.

"Until you find me my magic," she said, leaning closer to the alchemist, "you will not be leaving my sight. Not for one second. And if I find out that this is all part of some big plan—if I find out that there *is* no magic . . ." She laughed humorlessly, her eyes glittering. "Then there is certainly no magic strong enough to help you. Do we understand each other?"

"There is magic," the alchemist squeaked. "I swear. The greatest I have yet produced."

"Good." The Lady Premiere pulled away. "Then we go to find it."

"But what about the boy?" the alchemist said. "Do we just let him go?"

The Lady Premiere had already turned and started for the street again, her long fur coat swirling around her ankles. "Do not trouble yourself about the boy," she said. "I have spies and guards and friends all over this city. He will be found. And when he is found, he will be . . . handled."

The way she said the word made the hair on the back of Mo's neck stand up, as though he had been tickled there by a dozen insect legs.

"Now come!" the Lady Premiere commanded, without looking back, and the alchemist scurried after her. Mo could hear their footsteps long after they vanished into the fog and he had closed the gates behind them, breathing a sigh of relief.

"All clear," he whispered, stepping back into the stone hut and ducking down to peer under his desk. But the little dark space was just that—dark, and totally empty. Mo straightened up, scratching his head again.

"Where on earth . . . ?" he started to say, out loud, before noticing that the cat door was rocking slightly on its hinges with a *tap-tap-tap*-ing sound.

Mo got down clumsily on his hands and knees, lifted open the cat door, and squinted out.

He looked just in time to see the boy with no hat round the corner at the end of the alley, and then disappear from view.

SEVEN

IT WAS WITH A SENSE OF RELIEF THAT PO SLIPPED back into the Other Side after its conversation with Liesl. Bundle seemed relieved too: The ghostly animal skipped happily in front of Po, flickering in and out of other objects they encountered, exploring, turning flips in the air, expanding suddenly into a shapeless black cloud and then re-forming itself, trying to make Po laugh.

But Po was still thinking about Liesl. The ghost had not meant to lie to her, but the lie had come, and with it, the stirrings of feelings and attachments long forgotten. Even after Po was back on the Other Side, feeling the dark pulse of the endless starry night all around it, slipping away on the gentle sighings of the wind and floating between black valleys and cold dark stars, the ghost could not shake the memory of Liesl's face, or the way she had trembled ever so slightly when she said, *Tell him I miss him*, or the look she had given Po after it had lied to her: a naked, happy look, like the face of the dew-coated moonflower that grew in abundance on the Other Side, white and crescent-shaped. Something about the girl moved something in Po, twisted the airy tendrils of its being in a way that had long become unfamiliar.

We mustn't go back to the Living Side anymore, Bundle, Po thought to Bundle, and felt Bundle's animal mind think back a simple agreement. Bundle agreed with everything Po thought. It was a very loyal pet.

It's just not right, Po said. *It's not natural. We are dead, after all. We don't belong there.*

Mwark, came the noise from Bundle's mind, which Po knew meant, *Okay, yes, you're right.*

And the live girl will be fine, Po thought. *She was fine without us before; and she will be fine now.*

Mwark. Whatever you say; of course.

I'll miss the drawings, though, Po thought.

Bundle was silent, turning floaty flips ahead.

Whether Bundle had once been a dog or a cat was, at this point, impossible to say. Sometimes, in the natural inquisitive tilt of its head, and the twitchiness of its tail, and the prick of its ears, it seemed very cat. Other times, due to its tendency to follow Po around everywhere and yelp excitedly at every shooting star or wisp of cloud dust, it seemed much more dog.

But whatever it was, one thing was clear: Bundle was a natural explorer. It liked nothing better than to discover some new and twisted corner of the universe, and then, suddenly, to disperse—blending momentarily into the new place, the new space, whatever it was, and returning to its loose and shaggy shape whenever its curiosity about the new thing had been satisfied. Since it could no longer smell or look or touch, it could learn only in this way: by blending.

When Bundle was tired, it liked to disperse into Po. Bundle could not climb into Po's lap because Po had no lap, so instead it climbed inside: It curled up inside of Po's Essence, and Po walked for a time with the secret knowl-edge of this other thing, this other being, glowing at Po's very center like a star burning in the middle of darkness.

Of all the miracles Po had seen in the time and space of its death, Po thought this—the absorption of another, the carrying of it—was the most bewildering and remarkable of all. Whenever Bundle separated again, Po was left with

an ache of sadness that reminded the ghost of the body it
had once left behind.

Let's go to our place, Po thought to Bundle.

Mwark, Bundle thought back.

Bundle and Po skimmed over the top of a glowing,
moonlit hill and came to a place where black water ran
between soft, pillowed, cloudy hills: a quiet, secluded place,
and one both ghosts knew well, and came to often.

There was another ghost sitting by the river, however,
and Po stopped short. Bundle let out a small yelp of surprise.
This was Bundle and Po's secret spot, exactly one third of
the way between the endless waterfall and star 6,789. Po
had never seen another ghost there, not one single time.

The new ghost had its back to Bundle and Po, and it was
muttering something. It must have only recently crossed
over, as even from the back its silhouette was very defined,
and very clearly that of a man.

As Po drifted closer, it heard the man saying, "If I could
only get back to that willow tree. I'm sure then I could find
my way home. Fifteen feet from the tree is the pond, and
up the short little hill is the house, where little Lee-Lee will
be waiting with her mother. . . ."

Po was stunned. All the atoms of its being flipped

simultaneously in a funny direction, so the ghost shivered from the inside out. Po had not been kidding when it told Liesl that the chances of seeing her father again were next to impossible: And yet, here her father was. In Bundle and Po's secret place, no less.

Po was so surprised it made a sharp whistling sound, and the ghost of Liesl's father started, and turned around.

"Oh, hello," the ghost of Liesl's father said. "I didn't hear you come up."

Po refrained from pointing out that ghosts stepped soundlessly, since they did not have solid feet to walk with. The man was obviously brand-new, and confused. His contours were extraordinarily clear; there was only the tiniest bit of smudging around his hair, making him appear to be wearing a dark hat. He brought his hand to his cheek and swiped.

Po had never seen a ghost cry before. There were no actual tears: just quivering little dark spots, like shadows, that pushed apart the atoms of Liesl's father's face, temporarily revealing the starry sky beyond. Ghosts, even the newest ones, just weren't held together very tightly.

"What are you doing here?" Po asked Liesl's father. Bundle drifted forward cautiously. The ghost-animal did not fully blend with Liesl's father, but it wrapped itself around the man's feet, a kind of ghostly version of smelling.

"I appear to have gotten lost." Liesl's father shook his head and looked down at the shaggy shadow-pet massed around his feet, and then up at the flowing black dust of the river, and the spinning planets beyond the massive white hill-clouds. "I seem to have been wandering forever, and I can't find my way back. . . ." He trailed off, squinting at Po. "Who are you?"

"My name is Po."

"I'm having trouble seeing you clearly. I must have left my glasses at home." Liesl's father patted the front pocket of his shirt, which was still there in silhouette, but barely. Clothes faded first on the Other Side. They had nothing to hold them together at all: no soul, no Essence, no Being. Clothes were just things, and things scattered into nothing quite easily. "My name is Henry Morbower. Perhaps if you came a little closer . . . ?"

Po floated a little closer, knowing it would not help.

"Ah, yes, that's better," Henry said, obviously lying, and then gave a little frustrated shake of his feet. "I seem to have stepped in some mud earlier," he said.

"That's not mud," Po said. "That's Bundle."

Henry squinted. "What?"

"Bundle. Bundle's just gotten around your legs. Bundle's an explorer. That's why I think it might be more dog. On the other hand, it really likes the constellation Pisces—fish, you know. So maybe it's a little more cat."

Henry said, "Er, yes—quite. Of course. I see." Although of course he did not see. He kicked more emphatically with his feet. Bundle detached from around his legs and drifted back to Po.

"That's better now," Henry said, and Po heard Bundle think *Riff*, which was a sound of disapproval. "Do you and, er, Bundle come this way a lot? Do you know this area well?"

Po thought of a tree shaking its leaves in the wind, and as the ghost thought this, about the shaking tree, it managed to shrug. "About as well as anybody knows it, I guess."

Henry's face lit up, and it was painful to see. It reminded Po of Liesl. "Wonderful! A native. Then you can help point me in the right direction. You can help me get home."

Po decided there was no point in beating around the bush. "You're on the Other Side," the ghost said firmly. "You are no longer with the living. You've crossed over."

Henry was quiet for a minute. Another little dark crease appeared in his forehead; through it, Po could see a spinning haze of planetary dust. Henry was falling apart, slowly but surely. He was blending. Soon he would be as Po was—part of the Everything. Po felt a strange mixture of sadness and relief. The ghost reminded itself that losing form was natural, and good, and the way things were in the universe. There could be no regret about it.

At last Henry shook his head. "I understand all of that very well," he said firmly. "I met the nicest woman—Carol, was it?—on my way over here. Explained everything to me; how she had died of the flu after going out in the middle of the night to scavenge for potatoes. The man behind her had been killed in a bar brawl. I never was a drinker myself, you know, for that reason. But all the same, I need to get home. I need to get back to the pond, and the willow tree, and my wife, and little Lee-Lee. They'll be worried sick about me, I can tell you that."

Po did not know quite how to respond. Perhaps crossing over had shaken up the particles in Henry's brain, the ghost thought. "I'm sorry," Po began again, more slowly. "I don't think you understand. You've died."

"I understand that perfectly well," Henry said, a note of briskness creeping into his voice. "What did I just tell you?"

"But—but—" Po struggled for the words it needed. It

was not used to having to speak so much out loud, and for a second it regretted ever stepping foot in Liesl's bedroom. "You can't go home. Home is on the Living Side. There's no way to cross back. Not really. Not for good."

Henry climbed to his feet. Or rather, Henry's ghost simply unfolded and was standing. Despite being new, he was getting the hang of things. Bundle took refuge in Po's Essence; Po felt the sudden presence of the little animal inside of him.

"My dear boy," Henry said, and then squinted again. "My dear girl—my dear—whatever you are—I may be dead, but home is wherever I built my life, and it is where I will go back in my death. Home is where my only child was born, and home is where my first wife, my love, was laid in the ground. She's not here, after all—in this place you call the Other Side, because if she were, she would have found me already. She is not floating around in the darkness somewhere, and I will tell you why. She is not here, because she is home, and home is the pond with the willow tree standing next to it, and dead, alive, or in-between, I am going home. Do you understand me?"

The whole time he had been speaking, his voice had gotten louder and sterner, and as a result, Po felt small and rather ashamed. Distant—so distant now!—memories returned to Po, the tiniest, vaguest memories of the smell of chalk and paper and the feel of its knees pressed under a desk. And strangely, because Po had Bundle's Essence inside of him, the ghost also felt other long-buried memories, of sharp voices and the shame of a puddle on the floor between its legs, a creeping, seeping puddle on a very nice carpet.

But when the ghost tried to focus on the memories, they evaporated.

"How do you intend to get there?" Po asked.

"My daughter will take me," Henry said. "She knows the way."

"She misses you," Po said, remembering its promise. "She told me to tell you."

"I miss her, too." Henry sighed, and at once all the sternness was gone from his voice. He shook his head mournfully, and then said in a whisper, "It was the soup, you know. I should never have eaten the soup."

"What?" Po was once again confused.

"Never mind." Henry refolded himself so he was once again sitting by the silent, swiftly moving river. Suddenly he looked defeated, and Po could see the darkness eating at the edges of his shoulders now, and down around his arms—could tell that the Everything was already starting to pull hard on Henry's soul. "Leave me now," Henry said. "I'm very tired."

"Okay," Po said, and then, remembering the other thing Liesl had taught him, said, "I am sorry you are tired."

"That's okay," Henry said. He did not look again at Po. He stared off at the stars, at the sky, at the universe bending and unfolding. "Once Liesl brings me home, I will rest."

EIGHT

MEANWHILE, IN THE DARK, TWISTED ALLEYS OF the Living Side, Will was running for his life.

He ran without knowing where he was going. He ran blindly, impulsively, cutting left and right, down foul-smelling alleys and streets so close and shadowed he could hardly see.

Plan, he thought. *I need a plan.* But his heart was beating so loudly in his ears he couldn't think.

He knew one thing for sure: He could not go back to the alchemist's studio. He could never, ever go back to the alchemist's studio for as long as he lived, because the alchemist would kill him, and that would be the End of that.

Will was used to the alchemist's temper. He had seen the alchemist scream many times, and go purple from fury, like he did the time that Will confused arrowroot for gingerroot in an extremely complex protection powder, thus rendering it completely useless except for the thickening of soups.

But he had never, ever been so terrified of the alchemist as he had been tonight, when the Lady Premiere had swept into her private apartments and commanded her attendants to "Leave us," seeming to bring to the room an arctic chill with those two words.

It had been clear just from the tone of her voice and her dark, furious, glittering eyes, that she had not summoned the alchemist to congratulate him, or thank him, or make him Official, and the alchemist had turned to Will with a look of such withering anger and hatred that Will had felt the very center of his being quiver and go limp. And though there had been a fire blazing in the corner of the room, his teeth had started to chatter again.

"Useless!" the Lady Premiere had thundered at the alchemist. Normally hearing the familiar insult turned against his master might have struck Will as amusing, but not at that moment. At that moment he knew only that something had gone horribly, horribly wrong, and that he would be blamed.

"Excuse me?" the alchemist had spluttered, eyes bulging from his head.

"I said, useless! I ask you to bring me the greatest, the most powerful magic of all, and instead you bring me a pile of ash." And she had snapped open the wooden box and revealed the pale ashes inside, as dead of magic, as cold, as the coldest, deadest root in midwinter.

That was when the alchemist had gone the white color of the very hottest part of a flame. For a moment he had been unable to speak. He had stood there and stared at the wooden box in her arms. Then he had turned to Will and pronounced a single syllable: "You."

And yet in that tiny, nothing word, five years' worth of hatred and disappointment and dashed hopes and blame had been compressed, so Will had felt as though he had been hit with a physical force, as though the word were a fist straight to his gut. And he had known then that his life with the alchemist was finished. That he would never again sleep in the cold, narrow cot directly underneath the chimney, or get up in the half-light to feed the fish with tadpoles, or grind dried mullet into a powder under the alchemist's watchful gaze, or measure a goat's tears into a beaker and then add exactly two drops of moonlight, no more, no less, to make a cream that could cure even the biggest pimples.

The alchemist had tried to explain: The Lady Premiere had received the wrong wooden box, obviously. The one she was holding was most certainly not the one he had sent her. And it had all come out—that Will had not gone straight to the Lady Premiere's, as he had been commanded to do, but had instead gone to Mr. Gray's first; that he had fallen asleep by the fire; and afterward, his dim and bleary recollection of the large sack pressed into his arms and the wooden box on the table (no—*boxes*—there had been two of them, almost identical), and how he had gone stumbling outside, eyes half-closed, without checking to see that he had the correct one.

But it had not been enough. The Lady Premiere had screamed, the alchemist had cursed Will to damnation, and Will had known that if he stayed, he would most certainly be killed.

So instead he had run, hiding in the little guard hut when he discovered that the front gates were shut and there was no possibility of climbing them, and then crawling out through the cat door at the first opportunity.

Plan, plan, plan. The word bounced around in Will's mind like a pinball. His breath tore at his throat. He was sweating now, and the collar of his shirt stuck to his neck. His heart throbbed painfully, and he knew he needed to rest. He ducked into a narrow alleyway to catch his breath and listened for sounds of shouting or the pounding of feet. But he heard nothing except the faint scrabbling of rats. Good. He had not been followed. Not yet, anyway.

He needed to leave town. He needed to get as far away from the alchemist, and the Lady Premiere, and her assortment of servants and henchmen and sympathizers, as possible. Of course he had nowhere to go, but that hardly mattered.

He was an orphan, taken on by the alchemist to be little better than a slave. Will had never, not once, had anywhere to go—not really.

He realized this for the first time as he was crouching in the alleyway, but the realization, instead of making him feel unhappy, made him feel strangely free. It was like walking into a room and hearing everyone go silent and knowing yes, it was true, they *were* all talking about you; and they had been saying that your feet smelled like rotting fish; but also that you didn't care.

So he would leave town. So what? He would go wherever he found himself, and there he would be.

He remembered, when he lived in the orphanage, how he and the other boys had sometimes sneaked down to the overpass to watch the trains chugging slowly into the train station. There had been a vagabond who lived by the tracks, Will remembered: Crazy Carl, who collected glass bottles. Carl had built a shelter out of a little-rusted-out train car that had been abandoned by the tracks. It had kept him relatively safe from the wind and the rain and the cold. Will wondered whether it was still there. He wondered whether *Carl* was still there.

There was, he knew, only one way to find out.

When his heart had gone back to its normal rhythm, he stood up and started out in the direction of the train station and the overpass. Tonight he would sleep. Tomorrow he would catch a train.

NINE

LIESL HAD JUST FALLEN ASLEEP WHEN SHE FELT
something stirring by the bed. She had the sensation of a
long finger brushing her cheek, and for one confused second
she believed herself a tiny child again, back at the pond by
the willow tree, pressed facedown into the velvet-soft moss
that grew above her mother's grave. Then she opened her
eyes and saw that she was, of course, in her little attic room,
as she had been for ever so long. Bundle's moonlight eyes
were blinking at her, and Liesl thought she heard a very soft
mwark directed into her ear.

Po was there as well, standing by her bed. For a dark
piece of shadow, the ghost looked very pale.

"Hello," Liesl said, sitting up. "I didn't expect you back
so soon."

Po did not say that it had intended never to come back at all. "I saw your father again," Po said. "I gave him your message."

In her excitement, Liesl went to seize the ghost's hands. Her fingers passed through a soft place in the air, and Po seemed to shiver. "You did? You told him? How did he look? What did he say?"

Po bobbed away from the bed a little bit. The touch had unnerved the ghost. Po could pass through brick walls without feeling a thing; it could disperse into currents of air without pain. But it had felt the girl's hands, somehow, as though she'd been able to reach in and pull at Po's Essence. Essence was not physical matter, Po knew. No one could touch it. No one could destroy it either; that was the nice thing about Essence.

People could push and pull at you, and poke you, and probe as deep as they could go. They could even tear you apart, bit by bit. But at the heart and root and soul of you, something would remain untouched.

Po had not known all this when he was alive, but the ghost knew it now.

"He said that he should never have eaten the soup," Po said, and waited to see whether this would mean anything to Liesl.

She scrunched her mouth all the way to her nose. "The soup? What soup?"

"I don't know. That's what he said, though."

"Did he say anything else?" Liesl asked impatiently. It was annoying that Po had crossed into the land of the dead, and back, only to deliver a message about an unsatisfactory meal.

"Yes." Po hesitated. "He said that he must go home. He must go back to the place of the willow tree. He said that he will be able to rest then. He said you would bring him there."

Liesl sat very still. For a moment she was so still and white Po was actually frightened, though he had never once been frightened of a living one before. They were too fragile, too easily broken and dismantled: They had bones that broke and skin that tore and hearts that gave up with a sigh and rolled over.

But that was the problem with Liesl, Po realized. She seemed in that moment, as she sat there with her thin blanket bunched around her waist, to be like a glass thing on the verge of breaking. And the ghost did not *want* her to break.

Bundle must have felt it too. Po saw the fuzzy animal shape grow fuzzier and then sharper, fuzzier and then sharper, as it tried unsuccessfully to merge with Liesl. This was the other problem with living ones: They were separate, always separate. They could not truly merge. They did not know how to be anyone other than themselves, and even that they did not know how to be sometimes.

"I must take his ashes to the willow tree," Liesl whispered suddenly, with certainty. "I must bury my father next to my mother. Then his soul will move Beyond." She looked directly at the place where Po's eyes should have been, if Po were not a ghost, and again Po felt the very core of its Essence shiver in response.

"And you must help me," Liesl finished.

Po was unprepared for this. "Me?" it said unhappily. "Why me?"

"Because you are my friend," Liesl said.

"Friend," Po repeated. The word was unfamiliar by this point. Something tugged at the edges of Po's memory, the faintest of faintest recollections of a bark of laughter, and the smell of thick wool, and the sting of something wet against its cheek. *Snowball fight*, Po thought suddenly, without knowing where the words came from: words he had not thought of in ages and ages, in so long that millions of stars had collapsed and been born in that time.

"All right," Po said. It had never occurred to Po that it would ever have a friend again, in all of eternity. "I'll help you."

"I knew you would!" Liesl went to throw her arms around the ghost and nearly toppled over, as her arms passed through nothingness and then back on herself. Then, all at once, she seemed to collapse from within. She slumped back against the pillows. "But it's no use," she said despairingly. "How am I supposed to bury my father by the willow? I'm not allowed to leave the attic. I haven't left the attic in months and months. Augusta says it's too dangerous. I must be kept here, for my own protection. And the door is locked from the outside. It's only ever opened twice a day, when Karen comes to bring me my tray."

Karen was one of the servants Augusta, Liesl's step-mother, had hired with Liesl's father's money. Karen trundled up the winding stairs twice a day, sometimes with as little as a tiny strip of the smallest, toughest meat—usually the scraps from Augusta's meal—and a thimbleful of milk.

Augusta had not seen Liesl herself in all thirteen months that Liesl had been in the attic, and although Augusta had three servants and had her hair done every other day, she was always complaining that Liesl ate too much and they couldn't possibly afford to feed the little Attic Rat any more than they were already giving her.

Po was silent for a bit. "What time does she bring up your tray?" the ghost finally asked.

"Before dawn," Liesl said. "I'm usually asleep when she comes."

"Leave everything to me," Po said, and Liesl knew then that picking Po to be her very best friend had been the right thing to do.

TEN

KAREN McLAUGHLIN DID NOT LIKE TO GO TO THE
attic. She disliked climbing three staircases, and then
another set of tiny wooden stairs, to get from the kitchen to
the door, particularly when she had to carry a tray with her.

But more than that, she disliked seeing Liesl. It gave her
a shivery feeling—the girl with her pale, pale face and enormous blue eyes, the girl who never cried or shouted or made
a fuss about being locked in the attic but only sat there, staring, when Karen came in. It gave Karen the creeps. It was
just *not right*.

Even Milly, the cook, said so. "It ain't natural," she liked
to say, as she poured a bit of hot water over a bouillon cube
for Liesl's soup, or pounded a piece of fat and gristle with a
large hammer so Liesl would at least be able to get her teeth

through it. "Little girls ain't made to be locked up in attics like bats in the belfry. It'll bring bad luck on us all, you wait and see."

Milly was always saying, too, that *something should be done*, though her declarations never went further than that. Times were hard, jobs were few, and people all over the city were starving. If the servants in Augusta Morbower's employ had to deal with the specter of a pale, small child who lived in the attic—well, there were worse things.

(That was the kind of world they lived in: When people were afraid, they did not always do what they knew to be right. They turned away. They closed their eyes. They said, *Tomorrow. Tomorrow, perhaps, I'll do something about it.* And they said that until they died.)

Privately, Karen suspected that Liesl was a ghost, as she was very superstitious. Everyone was superstitious in those times of grayness and dark, when the sun had long ago stopped shining, and the color had slowly drained from the world.

True, Karen did not know of any ghosts who ate, and Liesl was always cleaning her plate of whatever food was placed there, no matter how disgusting or half-rotten. And true, too, that on the few occasions when Karen had been forced to touch the girl (twice when she had caught a fever; once when some of the fish Milly had sent up had been spoiled, and the girl had been ragingly sick for a whole day), Liesl had felt solid enough. But all in all, seeing Liesl gave Karen an uncomfortable, prickly feeling she could not quite identify: a feeling that reminded her of the time she had been caught by the nuns at her school stealing a chocolate chip cookie from Valerie Kimble's lunch basket—a feeling of being watched, and judged.

That was why she so dreaded her twice-daily trips up the narrow attic stairs, and why, as much as possible, she tried to come only when she knew the girl would be sleeping.

It was just after five thirty in the morning when she began making her way carefully up the stairs, balancing the tray, which today contained a bit of bread mixed with hot water to form a pasty porridge, and the usual few sips of milk. The house was even quieter than usual, and the shadows seemed to Karen particularly strange and black and huge. Suddenly she felt something brush her ankle and she jumped, nearly dropping the tray; a cat meowed in the darkness and she heard the scrabbling of paws on the wood, moving past her down the stairs. She exhaled. It was only Tuna, the mangy cat who had been informally adopted by the kitchen staff and who occasionally roamed the house at night, when Augusta wasn't around to give him a swift kick in the belly.

"Nothing but a kitty," Karen muttered to herself. "A little bitty kitty." But her heart was hammering, and she felt sweat pricking up under her arms. Something was wrong in the house this morning. She felt it; she *knew* it.

It was the ashes, she realized: that pile of ashes sitting in the wooden box on the mantel. It wasn't right; it wasn't *natural*. Like having a dead person propped up in the living room. And didn't ghosts always hover around their bodies? Even now, the master of the house could be watching her, tiptoeing up the stairs, ready to wrap his dark and ghostly fingers around her exposed neck. . . .

Something brushed against her cheek, and she cried out. But it was just a draft, just a draft.

"No such thing as ghosts," she whispered out loud. "No such thing as ghosts."

But it was with a feeling of dread and terror that she climbed the last three steps to the attic and carefully unlocked the door with the large skeleton key she kept in her apron pocket.

Several things happened quickly, one right after the other.

Liesl, who was sitting up in bed, not lying down with her eyes closed as she should have been, said, "Hello."

Po, standing directly next to her in the darkness, concentrated with all its might on distant memories of something vast and white burning high up in the sky, and its outline began to glow like a star peeking out against the darkness: faintly at first, then clearer and clearer, the outline of a child whose body was all made of blackness and air.

Po said, "Boo."

Bundle went, *Grrr*.

Then:

Karen dropped her tray.

Karen cried, "God help us!"

Karen turned and went running down the attic stairs as quickly as she could, a little noise of utter terror bubbling from her throat.

And:

In her haste, Karen forgot to lock the door behind her.

"Quickly," Po said to Liesl. Liesl flung away her covers and stood up. She was not dressed in her thin nightshirt, but in trousers, a large, moth-eaten sweater, an old purple velvet jacket, and regular shoes. She had not worn anything but slippers in so long, she had difficulty walking at first.

"We don't have much time," Po said, skating silently in front of her. The effort of appearing to the servant girl had been tiring, and Po allowed itself to ebb back to its normal shadowed state. "Hurry, hurry." Bundle zipped back and forth, materializing in various corners, and then briefly on the ceiling, in its excitement.

"I'm hurrying," Liesl whispered back. She slung the small sack she had packed earlier—containing a change of clothes, her drawing supplies, and a few odds and ends

from the attic—over her shoulder, and moved carefully to the door. A feeling of fear and wonder swept over her. It had been ever so long since she'd been out of the attic. She was almost afraid to leave it behind. She could no longer remember clearly what was on the other side of the door; what it felt like to stand outside, in the open air. She did not know how she would manage with no money and no clear idea of where she was going, and for a moment she thought of saying to Po, *I've changed my mind*.

But then she thought of her father, and the willow tree, and the soft moss that grew over her mother's grave, and instead she said, "Good-bye, attic," and followed the ghost's dark shape out of the door and down the stairs.

And while Karen was babbling to Milly in the kitchen, and Milly was fussing and murmuring, "Calm down, calm down, I can't understand a word of what you're saying" and wondering, privately, why every single servant had to be either a drunk or completely off her rocker, a little girl and her ghostly friend and a small ghostly animal were taking from the mantel in the living room a wooden box containing the most powerful magic in the world, and afterward stealing with it out into the street.

PART II

NARROW ESCAPES &
EXCITABLE SPARROWS

WHEN LIESL FIRST STEPPED OUT OF THE HOUSE, she drew a sharp breath, and Po had to urge her forward.

"Come," the ghost said. "Before we are discovered."

So Liesl followed the two shadows—the larger, person-shaped shadow and the smaller, animal-shaped shadow—down the path and through the iron gates and out onto the street. But there again she had to stop, overwhelmed.

She said, "It's so big. Bigger than it looks from the attic. I had forgotten." She didn't mean just the street, of course. She meant the world—roads, intersections, lefts and rights, twists and turns, choices.

Over the months Liesl had watched several baby sparrows hatch and grow in the little nest just outside of the attic window. She had always been particularly fascinated by the birds' first teetering steps to the edge of the roof: awkward, ungainly, and childlike, they looked like toddling children. And then suddenly the baby sparrows would launch into the air as their parents twittered their approval.

She had always wondered at the bravery of it. The sparrows jumped before they knew how to fly, and they learned to fly only because they had jumped.

Liesl felt a bit like a baby sparrow, standing in the cold, dark, empty street, with the city spread all around her and the world spread all around the city: as though she was perched in the bright, empty air with nothing to hold her.

"Where to?" Po asked Liesl.

They needed to find the train station, Liesl knew, because trains led out of the city of Dirge, to places of willow trees and lakes. Her head was full of birds. She pictured the men she had often watched from her window, striding toward the city center, their greatcoats flapping behind them like crow wings. Important men going important places, carried back and forth by great, chugging trains. She imagined them in her head; she mentally retraced their footsteps.

"This way," she said to Po, and pointed.

Bundle led the way, followed by Po. When the two ghosts had already crossed the street and melted into the shadows on the other side, Liesl found that her legs still wouldn't move. She thought, *Forward!* She thought, *Jump!* But nothing happened.

Po, noticing that Liesl was still standing there, frozen, returned to her.

"What are you waiting for?" the ghost asked.

"I—" At the last second, Liesl could not tell Po she was scared. "I forgot to say thank you," she said finally.

Po flickered. "Thank you?" it repeated. "What is that?"

Liesl thought. "It means, *You were wonderful*," she said. "It means, *I couldn't have done it without you*."

"Okay," Po said, and began skimming away again.

"Wait!" Liesl reached out to take the ghost's hand and felt her fingers close on empty air. She giggled a little. "Oops."

"What is it now?" The ghost was barely controlling its temper.

Liesl let out another snorting laugh and covered her mouth to stifle the sound. "I wanted your help crossing the street," she said. "I keep forgetting you aren't real."

"I'm real," Po said, bristling. "I'm as real as you are."

"Don't be mad," Liesl pleaded, and as Po floated off, she put one foot in front of the other without even noticing it. Step, step, step. "*You* know what I mean."

"I just don't have a body. Neither does wind or lightning, but they're *real*."

"It's only an expression, Po." Liesl had crossed the street. "Sheesh."

"Light doesn't have a body," Po continued, and up ahead, Bundle yipped and skipped and turned full circles in the air. "Music doesn't have a body, but that's real. . . ."

"For someone with no body, you're very *touchy*, you know."

A lone guard, returning from a long, cold shift at the residence of the Lady Premiere, heard voices and, pausing at the entrance to his building, saw a pretty girl carrying a knapsack and a wooden box, babbling happily to herself while beside her shadows shifted and swayed.

The guard thought, *Such a shame, when madness strikes in one so young. But that's the way of the world now.* And then he stepped inside and closed the door.

The girl and her ghost-friend continued down the street, moving toward the center of the city, arguing, while Bundle slipped and slid and floated beside them.

They argued and walked, walked and argued, and got farther away from Highland Avenue, and #31, and the attic.

Perhaps that was how the sparrows did it too; perhaps

they were looking so hard at the peaks and tips of the new rooftops coated with dew, and the vast new horizon, that they only forgot that they did not know how to fly until they were already in midair.

TWELVE

MO DID NOT GIVE MUCH THOUGHT TO THE PRETTY, babbling girl he had seen in the street. He was distracted.

Even after he had climbed the stairs to his apartment, and removed his coat, and changed into his warm thermal pajamas, and released Lefty from the fabric sling he used to carry her back and forth to work, and poured her a saucer of warm milk—even then, he could not stop thinking about the small, hatless alchemist's assistant with the chattering teeth.

Mo often felt his brain was like a big tin can, mostly full of air. Ideas tended to bounce around aimlessly there, clattering and making a lot of noise. Causes got mixed up with effects and vice versa, and he was never quite able to puzzle things through. Often he started thinking the beginning of a sentence but got lost by the time he had to reach its end.

Swiss cheese, his mother had always said of his brain. *Full of holes where things just go dropping out.*

But every so often an idea got lodged in the cheesy, melty part of his brain—a stretch of cheese without holes—and when it stuck, it was stuck good and permanently.

The idea that was stuck there now was: *The boy should really have a hat.*

Mo wondered whether the boy had found a nice, dry place to spend the night. He hoped so. If he had had more time, he could have told the boy about the gardening shed behind the First Boys' Academy, and the basement of St. Jude the Divine.

He knew all about the sneaky, hidden places in the city: cupboards and alleyways, rail stations and closets, underground tunnels and abandoned sheds. He had spent years searching the city for Bella, even after everyone had said it was hopeless—even after everyone had said to give up, move on, forget about her. His mother and father had looked for her too, until they had given up as well, each in turn, finally and forever: dying exactly a month apart of twin broken hearts.

A nice, big hat with earflaps. That'd fix him up.

Mo scolded himself as soon as the thought presented itself. The boy was no concern of his, as the tall, thin alchemist with the ugly dripping nose had pointed out to him. His landlady, Mrs. Elkins, always said he needed to learn to mind his own business and stop sticking his nose where it didn't belong. Curiosity killed the cat and so on and so forth.

"You're always trying to save everybody," she had said, frowning at him, when he had once again been late on the rent because he had given his last ten dollars to a beggar on the corner. "Most people don't want to be saved. Besides, if you keep bailing everybody out, they'll never learn to paddle on their own."

She was very smart, that Mrs. Elkins. He *was* a soft-headed, silly-hearted fool about people and things in trouble. Everybody had always said so. And one day it would all come to no good. Everybody had always said that, too. It was like the time he had rescued all those stray cats and dogs from the street. What had happened? They'd nearly clawed one another to death, all those wild street animals living in the same tiny two-room apartment, and in the end he'd had to give them all up to the pound when the neighbors complained. He'd had nothing to show for that experiment but a hundred pounds of half-eaten dog food, and fleas in the carpet.

Exactly right; exactly right. Give a man a fish, and he eats for a day; teach a man to fish, and he eats for a lifetime.

"Fish . . ." Mo said out loud, and then, because he had been reminded, went to his tiny kitchen, found a can of tuna fish on one of the two almost bare shelves above the small gas stove, and opened it carefully so that Lefty, who had eagerly slurped down her milk, would have something more to eat. The cat mewed and twitched her tail and twined herself between Mo's legs, and Mo said, "Patience, my girl. Be patient with old Mo."

When the tuna had been placed in Lefty's saucer, Mo got into bed. His little room was very drafty and he pulled his blankets all the way up to his chin, squeezed his eyes shut, and tried to think of dreamlike things: pink elephants; warm water with sunlight glinting off it; a mermaid reaching up to take his hand, saying, *Come, come down with me.*

He heard a series of small pinging noises against his window, and the mermaid vanished. He was alert again. It had started to hail.

Lots of rain and snow coming this week, the guard thought. *The boy will be cold* and *damp.*

A nice, big hat: one that fitted over those floppy ears of his.

It was no use. Mo knew he would not be able to sleep. He pushed away his thin blanket and stood. His room was very bare. There was just the small single bed, and a wooden table, and two chairs, and a narrow closet. Mo went to the closet and pushed aside all three of his uniforms, each neatly pressed, and extracted a small wooden box, with faded pink and blue flowers stenciled all around its side.

Inside this box was a necklace made of seashells (clasp broken), and a small yellow-haired doll (one eye missing), and a single mitten, and a large knit hat, and the smell—faint; faint, but still there—of raspberries.

Mo removed the hat that had once belonged to his sister, closed the box, and replaced it in the closet.

(We will close the box too, on the lost girl Bella. Some stories are meant to stay private.)

Outside Mo's window, the sky was a lighter gray now. Dawn would come in an hour or so. But it would not be any warmer. No. The air would be like the cold, thin bite of a razor.

Mo redressed quickly and placed the hat in his coat pocket.

"Better now, Lefty?" Mo said, and Lefty, full of milk and tuna fish, purred and rubbed against his ankles. Mo reached down and lifted her carefully into her sling, and placed the sling over his right shoulder and around his neck, and felt the cat's warmth against his chest, and smiled to himself.

He supposed his meddling didn't *always* come to no good. His terrible experiment with all the stray dogs and cats had, after all, left him with more than just fleas and a bunch of dog food. He still had Lefty.

Then he stepped out of his apartment and locked it behind him, and went off in search of the alchemist's assistant, while his imperfect and hole-riddled brain continued sending the same message to his oversized and perfectly functional heart.

The boy should really have a hat.

THIRTEEN

LIESL STOPPED IN THE MIDDLE OF THE TRAIN
station, overwhelmed by an impression of movement and
life: people everywhere, and sound, and trains flowing in
and out of the station like metal rivers. Life, flowing and
flowing and flowing.

"Which way?" Po and Bundle shimmered next to her.
In the bright, high lights of the station, they were nothing
more than snatches of silvery gray, occasional glimpses, like
the quick flash of a fish's belly moving under a river.

Dirge was a coastal city; south led to the ocean, east led
to a single, small fishing town and then to the ocean. That
left west and north.

Now that Liesl was out of the attic, it was easier for her to
climb down the towers of memory. She closed her eyes and

thought of snow peaked high like whipped cream (*ineffable snow, snowy peaked f's,* her mind said). She thought of the taste of ice melting on her tongue, and two spots of red on her father's cheeks, and the stamping of boots, and the smell of wood fire.

"North," she said.

Po became more visible for a moment as it studied the departures board intently. "Train 128," the ghost said. "Leaving from platform 22 in ten minutes. Northbound."

Liesl suddenly remembered that things cost money in the world. The whole world, in fact, was built on scraps and scrawls of paper. "I have no ticket," she said, her heart sinking. "And no money for one either."

"Don't worry," Po said. "I will teach you to be invisible. The trick is to think like a ghost."

Liesl looked unconvinced.

Po explained, "Think of dust and shadows and slippery, slide-y things that no one notices."

So Liesl did. She thought herself down into the spinning dust on the tiled floor, and away into the shadows, and so she and her ghostly friends passed unnoticed by the large man in an official-looking uniform who was checking tickets at the entrance to platform 22, just behind a large brood of shrieking, squawking children, and a harried-looking mother who kept saying irritably, "I dunno how many there are. Stopped counting after six, and *you* can go on and take one if you're so interested in 'em."

Will, meanwhile, was just arriving at the train station, full of hope for the future.

He had woken up an hour earlier, stiff and sore and hungry. His fingers ached with cold and his stomach was growling. But at least the little shed by the underpass had kept him relatively warm, and protected him from the rain and sleet and damp.

When he had arrived the night before, numb with exhaustion, he had seen no sign of Crazy Carl. The shed was swept clean and smelled strongly of wood planks and, strangely, like boiled meat—not altogether an unpleasant combination. He had curled up in a ball in the most deeply shadowed corner and immediately fallen asleep.

All in all, he had slept surprisingly well. The floor was not much harder than his cot at the alchemist's, and there had been no alarm clocks screaming shrilly and dragging him into consciousness, or nightmares of bulging fish with glassy eyes and disapproving voices calling him useless.

Will had started off for the train station in a very good mood, considering the fact that he was homeless, poor, hungry, and, he figured, a kind of outlaw. His mood improved tenfold when, just before arriving at the station, a carriage spun by him in the street and he was nearly clobbered in the head by a baked potato, which came flying out the window, wrapped neatly in wax paper, still warm and oozing with butter, with only a single bite removed from one of its sides.

Will almost cried as he sank his teeth into its soft, pillowed, buttery flesh. The people in the carriage must have been very rich. No one threw out food anymore.

He arrived at the train station full, and warm from his walk. He would go west, he thought. That's what people seemed to do. He saw on the departures board a train that was due to leave in an hour and a half. In the meantime he wandered through the train station, enjoying the echo and clatter of so many feet on the tiled floor, and the vast, cavernous ceiling looming far above him, and the flat gray light coming through the windows, and smells of coffee and sweat and perfume and wool and winter, and women sweeping by in elegant coats, and men striding past looking serious and important.

And the trains! The chugging, heaving, huffing, puffing trains, coming in and out of the station, shooting off to places unknown. Will had always loved trains. He felt he could stand there and watch them all day.

One of the trains, a northbound one, was getting ready to take off from platform 22, so Will made his way there to watch it depart. He noticed with pleasure the bitter stink of fire and coal, and the great bellowing of its horn, and the voice of the conductor calling, "All aboard! All aboard!"

Dimly, Will was aware of another voice shouting. This voice said, "You! Hullo! Hi! You there! With the ears!" But he was admiring the train's shiny red exterior, and handsome polished rails, and did not listen too closely to the other voice.

Then a hand came down heavily on his shoulder, and Will almost jumped out of his skin.

"There—you—are." Mo was panting heavily. The exertion of running to catch up with Will from the other side of the station had been particularly unpleasant because (1) Mo had not been required to move quickly in a very long time, and (2) Lefty, who was getting jostled by the movement, kept clawing him in dissatisfaction.

Will was struck head to toe by an icy-cold terror. He recognized the guard immediately; it was the man who had been outside the Lady Premiere's house. Of course he had been sent by her orders. Now Will would be arrested and brought back to the alchemist, to be tortured and killed.

The terror was blackness; and hatred, too. The guard had promised to keep Will's secret safe. He had seemed like a friend. Now the crushing weight of his hand made Will's shoulder ache. Will knew he could not hope to fight the guard and win. He was enormous; his forearm was the size of a normal neck.

Mo continued struggling and gasping for breath. Perhaps, he thought, he should lay off the hot chocolate. Or cut down—maybe to three or four cups a day, tops. His uniforms had seemed a bit tight recently. He could barely puff out, "Thought—might—find—here. Runaways—go—train—first."

"Last call! Laaaast call!" the conductor was hollering, and in that urgent, desperate moment Will imagined himself flying away from the station, soaring off forever in a train fitted with wings. There was a squealing and a screeching as the conductor released the train's brakes, and the locomotive began grinding forward, out of the station.

"Worried—you—getting—on—train—"

Mo bent over and placed his hands on his knees to

help him breathe more easily. In doing so, he let go of Will's shoulder.

Will did not hesitate for even a fraction of a second. Instantly he spun around and began to run, wildly, ducking and weaving through the crowd.

"Hey!" he heard the guard shout. "Hey! Come back here!"

Will no longer cared about going west, or north, or east, or south into the ocean. All he cared about was getting *away*. He collided with a woman carrying a small, dark poodle in her arms. The poodle let out a yelp, and the lady said, "Excuse you," but Will didn't stop. Ahead of him, the northbound train was gathering speed. If he could just make it . . . If he could pull himself up into the last car . . .

"Hey! Hey! Stop it right there!"

"That guard wants a word with you," said a man with a stiff white mustache, stepping in front of Will. Panicked, Will spun around him, twisting his ankle in the process. Pain ripped through his leg every time he put weight on it, but still he kept running. He was gaining on the train now, gaining on it. . . . Just a few more steps . . .

Sparks flew beneath the train's grinding wheels. Will could feel heat roaring from its engines.

"Somebody stop that boy!"

If only, if only, if only . . .

Will took two leaping steps forward and swung out wildly with his arm, and found his fingers closing around a door handle. He pulled, and his feet dragged, and then skimmed, and then lifted. And then he was on train 128, and looking back from the door in the very last car at the small, receding shape of the guard, who was standing on platform 22, frantically waving a small piece of fabric—which looked, from a distance, very much like a hat.

FOURTEEN

IT WAS ALL FINE AND WELL TO PRETEND TO BE invisible for one minute, or two. But Liesl was not invisible, unlike her ghostly friends, and as soon as she sat down in a comfortable seat in one of the very first cars, resting the heavy wooden box beside her, people began to give her strange looks. She was young to be traveling on her own, they thought. It was unusual. It was Not Right.

It did not help when Liesl began murmuring to herself (or so it seemed to them; for when they saw a flicker or flash or shimmer of light, they thought, *Trick of the eyes* instead of *Ghost* or *Magic*). She said, "I know, I know," when Po whispered, "People are staring."

She said, "Well, what do you want me to do about it?" when Po suggested she try being less conspicuous.

The other people in the train car—older people with pinched faces and bad tempers—saw a young child all alone, who talked to herself and kept stroking a plain wooden box as though it contained a very powerful magic (which, of course, it did, though even Liesl didn't know it).

Finally an old woman carrying a cane leaned over and said to Liesl, "Where are your mommy and daddy, little one?"

"They are both dead," Liesl answered truthfully. "My father is here." She tapped the wooden box. "I am taking him back to the willow tree, so he can rest."

This was an honest answer; unfortunately, it did not do anything but convince the old woman that the little girl was quite out of her mind. And if there was one thing the old woman with the cane disapproved of, it was people who were Not Right in the head.

"Yes, yes," the old woman murmured soothingly, while drawing back a few inches and wondering whether there was a policeman onboard. "I see. That box must be heavy. You look very tired."

"I am," Liesl said. "Very tired. We had to walk a long way."

"We?"

"Me and Po." Liesl pointed to the empty air beside her. "And Bundle, too. Though they don't get tired. Not like I do, anyway. Ghosts don't, I suppose."

"Ghosts, right,"

the woman said faintly. "No, no, I wouldn't imagine they do get tired." She forced her lips into a tight smile, thin as a strip of lemon rind. "I'm going to go get you a muffin, dearie, from the man with the snack cart. Would you like that? A nice potato muffin?"

Liesl had not realized just how hungry she was until that moment, when she imagined a steaming hot potato muffin. "Oh." She could barely swallow, her mouth was suddenly watering so much. "Oh, yes. I'd like that very much."

"Now you just wait here." The old woman stood up. "Sit tight. Don't twitch a muscle. I'll be back in a flash."

"Thank you," Liesl said, truly grateful.

As soon as the woman had swished down the aisle to the next train car, Po said, "I don't trust her."

"What are you talking about?" Liesl was tired, and starving, and irritated by Po's know-it-all attitude. "She's going to get me a muffin." She added, pettily, "You're just jealous you can't taste things anymore."

Po did not respond to this. "Wait here," the ghost said. It folded itself away and was gone. As soon as Po left, she was sorry she had said the thing about taste. That brief, empty pocket of air had reminded her of how alone she was without Po—so very, very alone. She had nobody at all, really.

Then she felt a shivery velvet sensation. Bundle was nuzzling her lap, inasmuch as ghosts could nuzzle. She felt a little better.

Po was back almost instantaneously. "Quickly," the ghost said. "She has gone to find a policeman. They are coming this way." Po added, because it thought the fact was relevant, "The man is big, and has badness in his Essence."

Liesl didn't know anything about Essence, but she did know about large police officers, and shiny handcuffs, and jail cells, and the fact that it was a crime to be riding a train without having paid to do so. She went very pale; almost as pale as the ghosts in books (books that don't know how ghosts really look).

"What should I do?" she asked. She was already picturing a tiny stone cell buried underground, which would be worse, so much worse, than the attic. And what would become of her father's ashes then? She picked up the wooden box and clutched it protectively to her chest. Next to her heart, through the wood, magic shimmered and swirled, though she could not feel it. Her heart was beating too loudly.

"We must hide," Po said.

Bundle jumped and evaporated temporarily into the air with a small, excited *mwark!*

Liesl inched out of her seat, clutching the wooden box to

her chest. The train lurched and bumped. She tightened her grip, swaying a little as she moved into the aisle. At the far end of the car she saw the old woman, coming toward her, the sharp metal tip at the end of her cane making a horrible *clack-clack-clack* noise with every step. Behind her was, as Po said, a very large and very mean-looking police officer wearing a bright blue uniform. To Liesl's horror, he already had a pair of handcuffs out, hanging loosely in his massive fist.

"There she is," Liesl heard the old woman say, in her high, lilting voice. "Quite off her rocker."

"Come on," Po said. The ghost was silent for a minute, and then it said, "Bundle will distract them." And then Bundle was twirling past them, back toward the old woman and the cop.

Although Liesl was so terrified she thought she might faint, she got the sense that Bundle and Po had just had a conversation without words, and in the midst of her terror she thought very clearly, *How strange. How strange and nice. To be able to always say what you mean without having to say anything.*

"Follow me," Po said, and began floating toward the back of the train.

Liesl moved quickly and carefully, desperate not to drop the wooden box, focusing on staying on her feet despite the jerky movements of the train. She did not dare look behind her, but she could feel the old woman and the cop bearing down on her, hear the *clack-clack-clack* of the steel-tipped cane moving ever closer. She imagined the cold feel of metal around her wrists, and she said a brief prayer in her mind to no one in particular: *Please.*

Just then the *clack-clack-clack*-ing stopped. Liesl heard the old woman let out a little cry of surprise, but she did not pause or look over her shoulder.

"Through here," Po said. Liesl reached out and heaved open the doors that separated her car from the next one—hearing for one brief moment the deafening, clattering roar of the wheels on the track, feeling the whipping cold wind and watching the ground zoom by in the space between the two cars—and then stepped through.

The old woman and the cop had, in that time, recovered from the startling and curious sensation that had overwhelmed them all at once: a kind of velvet feeling that had wrapped itself around their throats, not frightening but totally unfamiliar, and had made them both think, separately and for no apparent reason, of pets they had had in their childhood.

Bundle, feeling quite pleased with itself, thought itself back to Po's side.

The lady and the policeman looked up.

The little girl with the imaginary friends and the large wooden box was gone.

Will had hidden in the bathroom until he was sure the ticket collector had already come through. Then he had settled comfortably in a little window seat in one of the last passenger cars, and was quite enjoying the landscape streaming by his window: flat brown meadows and high, purple mountains, capped with snow. He had never been out of the city before. The only mountains he knew were mountains of brick, and he had never seen so much open space. And bare and brown and dead as it was (things had long ago stopped growing), all he could think of was the freedom of it, and how fun it would be to spread his arms and run, run, run in all that open space.

He was so absorbed by the view that he did not notice the girl from the attic hurry past him holding a wooden box—the very wooden box that had started all his troubles, in fact, though he would surely not have recognized it, plain as it was.

He was busy staring at the mountains.

FIFTEEN

THE FIRST FREIGHT CAR WAS FULL OF THE SHARP, unpleasant smell of animal droppings, and packed with cages. On one side there were rows and rows of chickens; on the opposite side were dogs and cats, some in fancy carrying-cases with leather tags, some in bare little cages. The dogs swiped at the cats, the cats hissed at the chickens, and the whole car was filled with howling.

"Let's keep going," Liesl said.

The second freight car was dark and very cold and smelled like dust. It was crowded with boxes, trunks, crates, and suitcases, which were stacked every which way, in high, teetering towers that shook and swayed as the train rattled along. Liesl's breath escaped in clouds when she exhaled. But at least it was quiet, and she would not be bothered by the woman with the cane, or the police officer, or the ticket collector.

She scrunched down in the small space between two gigantic wooden trunks and brought her knees to her chest, placing the wooden box carefully on the ground just behind her feet. Po folded itself into the narrow space next to her, and Bundle hovered on top of a suitcase nearby, becoming a long black haze as it stretched out.

Liesl yawned.

"You must be tired," Po said. It had only just occurred to the ghost that Liesl had barely slept at all.

Liesl nodded. "Very," she said, and rested her chin on her knees.

The train rattled forward, and the ghost and the girl sat in silence for a few minutes. There was a single, high window above them. It let in a trickle of gray and murky light, and flashes of cloud-covered sky.

"How will we know when we are where we need to be?" Po asked.

Liesl thought. "I remember a city made of smoke and fire," she said finally. "That's where we must get off. From there, we take a long road out of the city. It goes west into

the hills. Beyond the hills we'll find the house, and the pond, and the willow tree."

"A city of smoke and fire?" Po's edges flickered. "That sounds like a place on the Other Side."

Liesl tilted her head in Po's direction. "Do you have cities on the Other Side?"

"Great cities. Bigger than any here. Cities of water and dust; and cities made from flame; and cold, dark cities at the very heart of the planets, built into old stone."

Liesl considered this. "What is it like to be on the Other Side?"

Po thought about saying, *It is like being everything all at once, and holding the universe inside of you and being held inside of the universe.* But it did not think Liesl would understand, so the ghost said, "It is hard to explain. Perhaps one day you will know."

Liesl chipped at the trunk in front of her knees with a fingernail. "Perhaps," she said. She wasn't sure if the idea excited or frightened her. "Do you miss being here, though? Do you miss the Living Side?"

She could tell immediately that she had offended Po. Its outlines became much clearer in the dark, temporarily surrounded by a sharp white glow.

"Of course not," Po said. "It isn't like that. It's a different way of being, that's all."

"But one is alive," Liesl pointed out gently. "And one is not alive." She knew Po must be lying, at least a little. Po was the one who had told her that ghosts who were not attached to the Living Side—at least a very little—went Beyond.

Po swirled upward from where it had been sitting, and floated over to the window. "When you go swimming and you put your head under the water," Po said, "and everything is strange and underwater-sounding, and strange and underwater-looking, you don't miss the air, do you? You don't miss the above-water sounds and the above-water look. It's just different."

"True." Liesl was quiet for a moment. Then she added, "But I bet you'd miss it if you were drowning. I bet you'd really miss the air then."

Po was silent for a bit. It flitted restlessly back and forth in the freight car: a flicker of dark here; a shadow on the ceiling there. Liesl was very sorry she had upset her friend and wished she could say something to make up for it, but her brain was fuzzy and sleep pressed at her eyelids and she couldn't think.

Then Po was next to her again.

"Did you bring your drawing paper, as I asked you to?" Po asked.

Liesl nodded.

"Show me," Po said. Its voice sounded strange to Liesl. Closer and also more alive, somehow, than it usually did. *Feeling*, Liesl thought. Po's voice was full of feeling.

She reached into her canvas bag and removed her sketch pad, and pencils, and the two drawings she had made for Po.

Po was quiet for another few beats, staring down at the drawings and the blank page in Liesl's lap.

"I want you to draw me the sun," Po said at last.

"I can't possibly," Liesl said, stuttering. "I—I don't remember what it looks like."

"Just try," Po said. "Try and remember."

Liesl drew a circle, hesitantly. Then she erased it and drew a larger circle, floating in the center of the page. But still it didn't seem right. It looked dull and stupid and empty sitting there, like an expressionless face. If only she could remember . . . It had been so long.

She closed her eyes and let her pencil hover over her sketch pad. She wound herself back and down the stairways of memory, and felt her hand begin to move. The train jumped and lurched underneath her, and when she opened her eyes, she saw she'd covered her paper with nonsense: Squiggles and what looked like leaping flames stretched away from the circle in the center of the page, radiating all the way out to its edges.

"I've ruined it," Liesl said, and went to tear the picture in two.

"No," Po said sharply. Liesl jumped. Po went on, more quietly, "It's good. It's very good." Then it floated to the window again.

Liesl knew then that Po *had* been lying: The ghost did miss the Living Side. She understood then, too, that everyone drowns differently, and that for everyone—even ghosts—there is a different kind of air.

Train 128 steamed past the blurry gray countryside, past cracked and blackened fields.

Will pressed his nose to the window.

Liesl tucked her chin to her knees and slept.

Bundle watched over Liesl.

Po was a shadow on the wall, unmoving.

The old lady with the cane finished searching all the passenger cars, then berated the policeman for letting the crazy girl with the wooden box get away.

Mo, drinking hot chocolate and reading the paper, sat

contentedly on an express train to Cloverstown, where he intended to intercept train 128.

Lefty licked dribbles of chocolate from Mo's beard with a small pink tongue.

The alchemist and the Lady Premiere arrived at the gates of 31 Highland Avenue, where they had determined the magic had been taken by mistake.

A black-haired thief on his way to Gainsville stole two silver pieces from the grave of a dead man.

Time ticked forward. Stars collided. Planets were born and died. Everywhere and in every fold and bend of the universe, strange and miraculous things happened.

And so it was, just then.

SIXTEEN

JUST THEN, TOO, AUGUSTA HORTENSE VARICE-Morbower, second wife of the late Henry Morbower, and stepmother to Liesl Morbower, was rounding the corner of Highland Avenue in her carriage.

Her daughter, Vera, sat across from her, pale and sickly-looking despite the powder on her face and rouge on her cheeks, which she never went anywhere without, looking a little bit like a wriggly tadpole clothed in fur and lace.

"For the last time, stop your squirming!" Augusta barked at her daughter.

"Sorry, Mama," Vera mumbled. She couldn't help it. She squirmed when she was uncomfortable, and her mother's temper made her distinctly uncomfortable.

She had been trying all morning to be as quiet and helpful

as possible—since her mother had wrenched her out of her bed before dawn with the chilling words, "The little snot is gone! Fled! Disappeared!"

But as they rattled through the city, watching the dawn bleed pale gray light through the streets without shedding any light whatsoever on where Liesl had run off to, her mother's mood only got fouler and fouler. Augusta screamed, and ranted, and pulled her hair, and swore. Everything was ruined, and terrible, and disastrous. Even the warm potatoes that the cook had prepared, and carefully wrapped in wax paper, were inedible, and Augusta had hurled her breakfast out of the carriage window in a rage after taking only a single bite.

Augusta could not have been more different from Vera: She was broad, and flat, and enormous, with a wide, coarse face and hands as thick as paddles. She, too, was dressed in fur and lace, but she gave the impression of a full-grown toad. It did not help that when she was angry, the two warts on her forehead seemed to swell in size, as though expressing indignation on her behalf.

And oh, was Augusta angry! She was furious. She was enraged. The warts looked frighteningly large. Even Vera shrank away from the sight of them.

Augusta feared that everything she had built—every single last shred of happiness and security, which she had had to wrestle and wrangle and tweak and pull and suck from life with all her strength—was on the verge of collapse. The big, lofty house at 31 Highland Avenue with all the obedient, silent, scurrying servants; the parties and the dresses; the fat feasts and the tables groaning under the weight of roasts and pies and puddings, when half the world starved; all of it would vanish, be snatched right from under her very feet were the girl not found.

Her marriage to Liesl's father had been a marriage of convenience. She had once been Liesl's teacher. She had hated the ridiculous little drip even then, of course, although she had done her utmost to hide it, and Henry Morbower was hoping Augusta would prove to be a good and decent stepmother to his only daughter. Augusta had realized right away that he would never love her. His heart belonged fully and completely to his first wife (a woman, Augusta thought sneeringly, who must have been as silly as she was pretty, for in all her portraits she was laughing—as though there were anything in the world to laugh about!—and wearing the simplest cotton dresses, though of course she could have afforded the richest satin gowns).

Augusta also knew, when she married Mr. Morbower, that he would never remake the will in her favor. Upon his death, the house and all the vast Morbower fortune—accumulated by Henry Morbower's grandfather, a titan of the early railroads—would descend entirely on little Liesl Morbower, pale and strange and undeserving though she was. (A stupid one, like her mother; as a small girl she had danced in the rain! Actually danced in it! Ruining a pair of beautiful silk slippers in the process! Stupid.)

It would have been simpler, of course, to kill both Henry *and* his daughter. But Augusta worried about arousing suspicion. The slow death of a middle-aged man is hardly likely to be attributed to poison, especially when the poison is administered teaspoon by teaspoon, a bit in the soup every day, over the course of a whole year. (Patience was one of Augusta's *many* virtues.) But a little girl is different, quite different altogether.

So Henry had gone to the hospital and, at long last, died, and Liesl had been locked in the attic, and for the sake of the lawyers and the bank managers, Vera Varice had become Liesl Morbower and taken control of a fortune so large that even Augusta would have trouble spending all of it in a lifetime.

But now Liesl (the little monster!) had slipped away, and the whole beautiful plan—perfectly crafted and shaped, as delicately whittled as a sculpture made of ice—was in danger of collapse.

The warts on Augusta's forehead swelled like the throat of a puffer fish, and not for the first time that morning, she gave vent to her frustration with a low roar.

"We must find her!" she cried.

"Yes, Mama," said Vera meekly.

"She will ruin us!"

"Of course, Mama."

"And stop agreeing with everything I say, you nitwit. You're only making it worse."

"As you say, Mama."

Augusta rolled her eyes and muttered a curse under her breath, and Vera shrank back and turned an even more unattractive shade of pale green.

"Stop!" Augusta bellowed suddenly to the driver, and the coach came to a shuddering halt in front of 31 Highland Avenue, where the Lady Premiere and the alchemist were standing with a very frightened-looking maid, who was speaking to them through the iron gates. With her head protruding from a gap in the iron latticework, the maid looked, thought Augusta, like a criminal who had been placed in the stocks.

In fact just then the maid would *rather* have been a criminal in the stocks—or a fish in a casserole, or a potato in a skillet. Anything would have been preferable to being Karen McLaughlin, who had, in the course of one morning, seen a ghost, accidentally turned loose the girl in the attic, and received a stinging paddling by her mistress for the error.

To make matters worse, there was now a very tall and very angry woman in a very long fur coat at the gates, screaming at her.

As Augusta prepared to descend from the carriage, she heard her maid stammering out apologies.

"I'm s-sorry, ma'am. Rules is the rules. And nobody—not even Lady Prematures—"

"Lady Premiere. *Premiere*." The Lady Premiere's eyes were nearly bulging out of her head. "Meaning that there is only one!"

"Right—er—not even a Lady Premiere can come in without Ms. Augusta's permission—"

"Permission that is most humbly granted," Augusta interrupted, sweeping out of the carriage and curtsying deeply in front of the Lady Premiere. The alchemist, watching her, had the impression of a very squat boulder tumbling toward him, and he shuddered.

Vera flitted uncertainly after her mother. Augusta elbowed her daughter sharply in the ribs, and Vera doubled forward in pain. The Lady Premiere mistook the gesture for a bow.

"To what," Augusta said, making her voice so sickeningly sweet it caused the coachman behind her to choke a little, "do we owe this enormous honor, Your Grace?"

The Lady Premiere was still shaking with rage. "Never," she sputtered and began again. "Never in my life have I been forced to wait outside. For anyone. At any time. Never have I been forced to stand on the street like a—like a—"

Words failed her. She was overwhelmed by the smell of cabbages cooking, and she closed her eyes tightly against the memories of the dingy home in Howard's Glen. Her ears filled with the distant sound of laughter and chanting: *Gross and rotten, wretched Gretchen!*

She snapped her eyes open. Those days were over!

"Like a commoner?" one of the Lady Premiere's servants, standing a little apart, suggested.

"Yes, exactly. Like a commoner." The Lady Premiere

had, in fact, forgotten the word. Just pronouncing it brought back the taste of sour milk and poverty and spoiled things.

"You'll have to forgive her," Augusta said smoothly, casting a withering glance at the maid—a glance in which the promise of another, even more serious, paddling was written. "She was dropped on her head quite frequently as a baby. Her mother was a hopeless drunk."

"Milly told me my mother was a good Christian woman," Karen said, her bottom lip quivering.

"She lied, obviously," Augusta snapped. "Now get inside, where you belong."

Karen scurried into the house, whimpering.

Augusta produced a large golden key from her purse, and with it unlocked the gates. She gestured grandly for the Lady Premiere to precede her into the yard. Inwardly, Augusta trembled with excitement. A visit! From the Lady Premiere! Who was a princess in her native Spain (or was it Portugal . . . ?)! It was outstanding! It was unheard of! The neighbors would seethe with jealousy.

She hoped they were looking out of their windows right now. She thought she'd seen the corner of Susan Salway's dining room curtains swishing. Good. Let Susan see her, Augusta Hortense Varice-Morbower, escorting the Lady

Premiere into her home. It would serve Susan right, for forcing Augusta to suffer her endless monologues about the accomplishments of little Jeremy and Josephine—as though those two sallow-looking creatures with the faces like the bottom side of a waffle iron were anything to boast about!

Augusta was slightly disappointed when she had to actually admit the Lady Premiere *into* the house, where the powerful woman could not be seen and admired.

Then Augusta had a dark thought: a thought so black it wrapped her in a momentary fog. This—the visit from the Lady Premiere, the envious looks, the golden carriage parked just outside her gates—was exactly the kind of thing she would lose if Liesl, that sniveling snot, were not found quickly.

In that moment, as Augusta bustled through the grand hallway with her guests, she came to a snap decision.

Risk or no risk, she could not have Liesl, the *real* Liesl, running around, ready to turn the life Augusta had earned—the life she deserved—to smoke.

No. It could not be. When she found the girl, she would kill her.

Augusta felt much better after coming to this decision.

"Would you like tea?" she asked brightly. "Coffee? Chocolate?"

"There is no time for that." The Lady Premiere sailed past her into the drawing room, as though it were her house and not Augusta's.

Once Augusta, the Lady Premiere, and the alchemist were safely seated—Vera having slipped away as soon as the opportunity presented itself—the Lady Premiere directed her penetrating gaze at Augusta. In that moment, Augusta couldn't help but feel a slight chill. Perhaps the *idea* of the Lady Premiere's visit was preferable, she thought, to the real thing.

"I will come right to the point," the Lady Premiere said. "There has been a terrible misunderstanding. You are in possession of something that belongs to me. And I am in possession of something that belongs to you."

"Oh?" Augusta was more than a little disappointed that the visit was not purely social—she had been hoping that this marked her ascension into the highest ranks of society—but she did her best not to show it. "And what is that?"

The Lady Premiere stared at the alchemist, who had, in the short time he had spent with the Lady Premiere, learned that it was best to remain absolutely silent and hope that she would forget you were there. When the alchemist did nothing, the Lady Premiere stepped on his foot, and he started nervously out of his chair with a yelp, producing, as he did so, a wooden box.

"I believe this is yours," the Lady Premiere said. The alchemist opened the box, and Augusta found herself staring at piles of soft ash. "His name was Henry, was it not?"

"I don't understand," Augusta said.

"That is your husband," the Lady Premiere said placidly. "Or, it *was* your husband. I imagine there was more to him when he was alive."

"There must be some mistake." Augusta was beginning to feel that the Lady Premiere was quite out of her mind. "The remains of my dear husband—rest his soul—are sitting right on top of the . . ."

Augusta trailed off in the middle of gesturing grandly toward the mantel, where she had been keeping Henry Morbower's ashes on the off chance that anyone important came by to pay respects. (She wanted to play the part of the grieving widow convincingly. Eventually, she planned to bury the box in the backyard, next to the turnips. Or perhaps she would just dump the ashes in the little servants' latrine out back. The wooden box itself was very nice, and could easily be reused.)

Now, she saw, the wooden box was missing.

Augusta made a strangled sound in the back of her throat. The sound turned into a high whine, which soon became a roar. Hearing the terrible sound, Vera came running into the room. She looked more like a sad tadpole than ever, now that she had removed her hat. Her brown hair was plastered listlessly across a large, shiny forehead.

"Is everything all right, Mama?" she ventured.

"Everything is not all right," Augusta croaked out. "Did you remove the wooden box from the mantel?"

"No, Mama. I haven't touched it."

Another rumble quaked upward through Augusta's expansive body. The warts on her forehead looked ready to explode. "Karen!"

Karen reappeared, her eyes red and swollen.

"Karen"—Augusta's eyes glittered dangerously—"where is the wooden box containing the ashes of my dear departed husband?"

Karen looked at the empty space on the mantel, opened her mouth once, closed it, and opened it again. "I don't know, ma'am," she croaked. "It was surely there this morning, when I did the dusting. Just before I brought up the tray and was attacked by the ghost." Karen regretted the word *ghost* as soon as it had escaped her lips. She had already been paddled once today for her silliness.

To the surprise of everyone in the room, the alchemist startled suddenly from his chair. He had gone a deathly white. "A ghost? You said you saw a ghost?"

"Never mind her," Augusta snapped. "I've already told you about the head trauma she sustained as an infant. Quite tragic." She turned toward the Lady Premiere and made a sipping gesture with her hand. "It was the whiskey that did it."

But Karen was inspired by the alchemist's response to her story. He believed her, she knew, and so she went on, "It was a terrible ghost. Enormous and evil-looking, with glowing red eyes." She was making this up, of course; but then again, the ghost really had seemed terrible and evil to her, so it wasn't exactly a lie. "He was just standing there next to the girl—the little girl—as though she had *summoned* it." Karen mopped her forehead with her apron. "Very unnatural."

The alchemist was trembling. He could not speak.

"A little girl?" the Lady Premiere said sharply. "What little girl?"

"Just one of the servants, who lives in the attic." Augusta tittered nervously. "Nobody to bother about. Skittish creature. She ran off early this morning. *Somebody* forgot to lock the door to her room." She glared at Karen.

"The girl!" the alchemist exclaimed wildly. "The girl has the magic. She has used it to raise a ghost. It is as the book promised. *It works. The magic works.*" He turned triumphantly to the Lady Premiere and performed a little skipping dance. "You see? I told you I would make you the most powerful magic in the world—a potion to raise the dead!"

"You seem to forget a minor detail," the Lady Premiere said sweetly.

"What's that?" The alchemist was still skipping his boots merrily across the rug.

"WE DO NOT HAVE THE MAGIC!" the Lady Premiere screamed. Across the street, there was the sound of shattering glass, and a dog began barking. The alchemist toppled backward into his chair. His face seemed to collapse on itself like a soufflé taken too early from the oven.

"Would someone kindly," Augusta said, wiggling her pinkie finger into her eardrum in the hopes that it would stop the ringing there, "explain what is going on?"

"It's the boy," the alchemist muttered darkly. "It's that useless, worthless, disgusting, vile shred of a boy. It's all his fault; I'd stake my life on it. He must have brought her the magic."

Augusta turned to the alchemist with renewed interest. She had never met the alchemist in person but knew of his work. In fact she had more than once sent a servant round to purchase one of his . . . concoctions.

Here, she thought, was a man who understood children.

"Useless, worthless, and disgusting, hmmm? That does sound like someone Li—um, my servant girl would know. The adjectives describe her most exactly."

"He brought her the magic *I* created—the product of nearly five years' work—and she has used it to reverse the Order of Things. She has successfully raised the dead."

"Raised the dead . . ." Augusta felt a flutter of fear beating behind her rib cage. If Liesl could raise the dead . . . and if she should somehow raise the ghost of her own father . . .

Augusta closed her eyes quickly against the image of a towering black shape, with eyes like two glowing red coals, pointing an accusing finger, thundering out, *Murderer!*

"I did often see a boy standing on the street corner at night, looking up toward the attic," Karen put in, desperate to redeem herself. "Looking quite lost. Muttering to himself, sometimes, and making signs with his hands."

"I knew it!" the alchemist spat out bitterly. "They are working together to ruin me. They are in cahoots! They are in collaboration! They are in cooperation! They are in collusion!"

"And you will be in solitary confinement if you do not shut up," the Lady Premiere snapped. She took a deep breath. It was apparent to her by now that everyone—the froglike woman in her ridiculous getup and that sad-looking slippery daughter of hers, the servant girl, even the alchemist—was a complete moron. She would have to take matters into her own hands. "Mrs. Morbower, this servant of yours. What is her name?"

Augusta's mind went blank for a moment. "Vera," she sputtered out.

The real Vera squeaked.

"Well, it is obvious, Mrs. Morbower, that this Vera and the alchemist's apprentice—"

"Former apprentice! He is most certainly fired!"

"*Former apprentice*"—the Lady Premiere gritted her teeth—"have conspired to steal a most powerful magic. Magic that, incidentally, belongs to me." She flicked an invisible speck of dust from her fur coat with a long, sharp fingernail. "This, of course, cannot be permitted. We must find them. The question now is"—she leaned forward—"*where have they gone?*"

The drawing room was silent but for the sonorous ticking of the large grandfather clock in the corner.

The real Vera, who was pretending to be Liesl, coughed. "Excuse me," she ventured, blushing a deeper green as four pairs of eyes turned instantly on her. "I found these today in

L—I mean, in Vera's room. When you asked me to search it this morning, Mama." She reached into her small fur-lined satchel and pulled out a handful of crumpled-up paper.

"What is this trash?" Augusta snatched the papers from her daughter's hands and smoothed them against her lap. Her face grew very still.

"I believe they are drawings, Mama," Vera squeaked. Then she added, "I think they are quite good." When to her surprise her mother did not tell her to shut up, or turn around and cuff her around the ears, she felt inspired to say, "That is a weeping willow tree, I believe, and beyond it, a pond. Quite realistic. My art teacher, Mrs. Gold, would say she had *l'oeil*. That's French, of course, and means—"

"Shut up!" Augusta hissed, and Real Vera shut her mouth quickly.

Augusta stared wonderingly at the collection of drawings heaped on her lap. She was surprised the girl remembered so accurately. It had been years since she'd lived in the Red House, which stood near the pond and the willow tree—exactly four years since Augusta had become her stepmother and insisted the family move into the city. Augusta had visited that awful, creaking place only twice, but that had been sufficient. She knew she could never live in that shambling, fallen-down mess—with its maze of small rooms and faded yellow wallpaper and slanty wooden hallways and smell, all the time, of wild heather. She shuddered to recall it. And why should she have lived in such a hovel, when Mr. Morbower could practically afford a palace!

She frowned. Yes, the first Mrs. Morbower had been most definitely soft in the head.

Liesl had been only seven years old when they moved: And yet here it was, every detail on the page, every blade of grass and leaf exactly where it should be. Remarkable.

Augusta realized that the alchemist and the Lady Premiere were both staring at her with thinly veiled impatience.

She stood up, folding the drawings as she did so and tucking them carefully into her purse.

"I have a very good idea of where she is," Augusta said grimly. "She is no doubt headed for Gainsville even now. And she must be gotten back." She added in her head: *And then, she dies.*

The Lady Premiere felt a sharp pulsing in her chest: Her heart, which very occasionally still made itself known, let out a few panicked movements. Gainsville was not far from Howard's Glen, and she had vowed never to go to that part of the world again for as long as she lived. But there was nothing to be done about it.

"We leave at once," the Lady Premiere said, and swept to the door before anyone could contradict her.

SEVENTEEN

PO WOKE LIESL SOMETIME TOWARD DAWN. FOR A moment she didn't know where she was. Then, as her eyes adjusted, she made out the looming shapes of the boxes and suitcases all around her, and recognized the musty smell and the lurching of the train car. Her hand went reflexively to the wooden box tucked behind her feet. Safe.

"Liesl, come look," the ghost said, then skated to the window. The sky was still a velvet purple dark, with just a thin line of gray ringed around the horizon.

Liesl stood up unsteadily. Her legs were cramping, and she was very sore. She navigated the teetering piles of luggage with difficulty and joined Po. By standing on her tiptoes on top of a hatbox placed on a wooden trunk, she was able to see out the window. She saw all the many train cars ahead of hers shaking and clattering and shimmying past the flat, dark fields that surrounded them, looking like a long metal snake.

"A city made of smoke and fire," Po said, with a note of excitement in its voice. It pointed with what would have been a finger, if it had had one.

Ahead, Liesl saw the rising spires of an approaching city. The buildings seemed to be built out of soot and blackness; a haze of smoke clung to them like a shroud, and everywhere high towers sent bright orange flames toward the dark sky, and belched terrible-smelling fumes.

"That is our stop," Po said, although the ghost made it sound like a question.

Bundle went, *Mwark*.

At that moment the train began to slow; the lurching began to lessen. A sign flashed briefly in the darkness. It read CLOVERSTOWN, 2 MILES.

"Yes." Liesl gripped the windowsill tightly, keeping her eyes on those leaping chimneys of flame and trying not to think of the safety and the closeness of the attic. "That is our stop."

* * *

Will had balled up his jacket to serve as a makeshift pillow and had slept most of the night with his head resting against the window. He woke up as the train was drawing into a station.

The conductor moved through the aisles, ringing a bell, bellowing, "Cloverstown! First stop, Cloverstown! This is Cloverstown!"

"He doesn't have to shout," someone muttered. Will started. He had not seen anyone sit down. An old woman, working a finger irritably in one ear and tapping her steel-tipped cane agitatedly, was seated across the aisle from him, next to an enormous police officer who continued to sleep, head to chest, snoring.

Will turned back to the window. He knew of Cloverstown. It was a factory and mining town. In the hills that surrounded it were the mines, where boys from the orphanage who had not found families or employment were ultimately sent, to work forever underground in those dark and terrible tunnels, burrowing like insects and living with the constant crushing fear of all that stone and earth over their heads, ready to come crashing down.

The girls went to work in the Cloverstown factories, sewing day in and day out, stitching cheap linens and hat linings until their eyes gave out and they went blind, or stirring large vats of poisonous chemicals until, one day, their minds went as soft as cheese that has been left too long in the heat. The end result was always the same: They ended up beggars, endlessly walking the filthy, teeming streets, begging money from people hardly richer or better off than they were.

For the first time, as Will stared at the awful black buildings—so coated with coal dust they looked like they'd been crafted from smoke—and heard the roar of the furnaces, he began to question his decision to leave the alchemist's. At least at the alchemist's he had had food (most of the time) and a roof over his head. He thought about the boys who had gone into the mines. He thought about the way they had shivered when the cart came to retrieve them from the orphanage, and the look of their sad, pale, defeated faces, as though they were already ghosts.

"Cloverstown! Cloverstown! First stop, Cloverstown! Next stop, Howard's Glen!"

"Enough to take your ear off," the old woman muttered, this time working her finger in her other ear.

Well, he would most certainly not get off in Cloverstown. He would keep going, he decided. He would go all the way north, to the last stop. Perhaps he could build a snow hut and live in it for a time.

And then the unthinkable, the unbelievable, the impossible happened: As Will was staring at the grimy Cloverstown station, the girl from the attic passed underneath his window, walking neatly and deliberately down the platform, carrying a small wooden box.

Will let out a cry of surprise and jumped up from his seat.

"It's her!" He was filled with such a tremendous, tumbling sense of joy he could not help but exclaim out loud, to no one in particular. "It's the girl in the attic. Only she's not in the attic anymore. She's here. Or, um, there."

"What are you babbling on about now?" demanded the old woman irritably, thinking that no one had the decency to speak at a normal volume. But she stumped to her feet and leaned toward the window to see what the scraggly boy was so excited about.

Liesl had at that moment paused outside to get her bearings, and as she turned and looked around her, both Will and the old woman, staring down, got a nice long look at her face. Will thought, *Angel*, precisely as the old woman thought, *Devil*, and let out a wicked howl.

(That is the strangest thing about the world: how it looks so different from every point of view.)

"It's her!" the old woman screeched. "The batty one!" She prodded the policeman forcefully awake with her cane. "Come on, now. Move it."

Will had already darted around her and was pushing his way toward the door, threading past the other passengers who were disembarking. His heart pounded painfully in his ribs. It was a sign! She was a sign—a sign he had made the right decision. He must, he absolutely must, find her.

The old woman and the police officer came clomping along behind him, but he took no notice of them.

"Excuse me, excuse me." He ducked past a frail man carrying an empty birdcage and burst onto the platform.

The spot where Liesl had been standing was empty. She was gone.

For a second his heart dived all the way to his toes. He had lost her. But then he caught a glimpse of a dark purple coat and a bit of straight brown hair, a little ways farther down the platform. Instantly he set out at a run.

"Wait!" he called out. "Wait, please! Wait for me!" He wished more than anything, now, he had had the courage to ask for her name. He began calling out all the girls' names he had thought of for her over the past thirteen months, hoping that one of them would be correct. "Rebecca! Katharine! Francine! Eliza! Laura!"

But she kept walking.

Dimly he was aware of the loud clattering of a cane behind him, and heavy footsteps, and a confusion of voices—one high and shrill and demanding, one a low growl—but he could think of nothing but the small figure in front of him.

And finally, when he was no more than ten feet away from her, he burst out, "You! The girl from the attic! Wait."

She stopped walking right away. He stopped running only a few feet away from her. He stood there, panting in the thick and smoke-clotted air, while the girl from the attic turned around—slowly, so slowly, it seemed to him. In the time it took her to turn around, he had time to think of all the things she might do when she saw him there. Her face would light up. She would say, "You—the boy from the street corner." Or somehow, miraculously (for she was a miracle to him; her presence there, on the platform, was proof), she would know his name, and she would greet him by it. "Hello, Will," or "Hi, Will," she would say.

But Liesl did none of those things.

Liesl turned, and saw a strange boy she had never seen

before, red faced and panting; and behind him, she saw the old woman who had pretended to be on her way to get a hot potato muffin when really she had gone for the policeman; and behind *her*, she saw the policeman with his sharp silver handcuffs in his hand. Her mind went *click-click-whirr*, and she thought, *Boywomanpoliceman*, one unit.

In her ear, Po spoke the word, "Run."

And so she turned and ran. She threw herself headfirst into the crowd, darting past fat women and squat children and men with dirty faces. She bumped up against a soft belly and heard a very quiet meow. She had collided with a man in a guard's uniform, carrying a cat in a small sling.

"Excuse me," Liesl said, always mindful of her manners. Then she took off running again.

The guard, who had managed to intercept train 128 thanks to an express train and a well-timed coach, and was standing on the platform waiting to board, took no notice of her. He was holding a hat, and staring determinedly at the small pink-eared boy who had just had his deepest dreams bashed to pieces.

Will was so distressed by Liesl's horrified reaction—so different from what he had imagined!—he did not immediately have the heart to pursue her. What, he wondered, had he done? What could have caused her to have so violent a reaction? Was it his hair? Had he yelled too loudly? Or perhaps (he cupped a hand in front of his mouth and sniffed) the potato breath?

The old woman clomped up behind him and dug her nails sharply into Will's shoulder.

"Where is she?" she demanded. She, too, was panting. "Where has she run off to?"

"What?" Will was still too devastated, and dazed, to think clearly. For over a year he had prayed to speak to the girl in the attic, and finally he had spoken to her, and she had run away! It was a cruel joke.

"The girl." The woman narrowed her squinty eyes at him, until they were no more than two brown-colored peas settled neatly inside the wrinkles. "Your little friend. The nutty one."

"She isn't nutty," Will said automatically, but immediately he began to have doubts. He didn't really know anything about her . . . and that *would* explain the running off. . . .

"She's as nutty as an acorn," the old woman scoffed. "She's as batty as a belfry! She's a public menace, and she needs to be locked up!" The old woman stared pointedly at the police officer next to her, who grunted in agreement. Will noticed, uneasily, that the police officer was holding a pair of handcuffs.

"I—I don't know anything about an acorn," Will said nervously. He tried to back away, but the old woman kept her hand on his shoulder. Her nails dug into his skin.

"You will lead us to her," she said, leaning closer, so he could see her yellow teeth very clearly. "It is your duty. It is for the Public Good."

"I—," Will started to protest, when a heavy hand clamped down on his *other* shoulder. Turning, he let out a squeal of disbelief, and the words died in his throat.

It was the guard from the Lady Premiere's house.

"There you are," Mo said cheerfully. "I had to follow you all the way from Dirge. You're a pretty slippery thing, you know that?"

Will tried to speak, but only managed to gurgle.

"Had to take the express," Mo continued, unaware that beneath his hand, Will had started to tremble violently. "Made it just by the skin of my coattails. I was just about to pop onboard when I looked around and saw you. Funny, isn't it?" Mo chuckled to himself.

"Excuse me," the old woman said witheringly. "I was having a conversation with this boy, and you have barged right into it."

"I beg your pardon, ma'am." Mo swept off his hat and

performed a little bow, all the time keeping his hand on Will's shoulder. "My name is Mo, and I am at your service." As he tipped forward, Lefty peeked his head out of the sling strapped around Mo's chest and let out a small meow.

The old woman shrieked. "What is that filthy animal doing on your—on your—" The rest of her words were swallowed by an enormous *"ACHOO!"*

"Lefty's not filthy," Mo said reproachfully. As he spoke, he tugged Will closer to him. "Might have a bit of sardine breath, of course, but other than that she's clean as a whistle."

"All cats are—*ACHOO!*—filthy." The old woman tugged Will back toward her side. "And I am deeply—*ACHOO!*—allergic, and demand that you—*ACHOO!*—get rid of that animal at once."

Tug. Will went back to Mo's side.

"With no disrespect, ma'am, I'd ask you whether *you've* had your bath today. Lefty has already had two."

Tug. Back to the old woman.

"If my 'bath' consisted of—*ACHOO!*—licking myself from head to toe to—to—to—*ACHOO!*—tail, we might be glad that I had not—*ACHOO!*—taken it!"

Lefty seemed to be quite enjoying the argument about

her cleanliness. Her tail, which protruded from the sling, was whipping merrily back and forth.

Will, sensing his opportunity to escape, sent a quick, silent apology the cat's way—*Sorry, girl, this might pinch for a minute*—reached out, grabbed the cat's tail, and squeezed as hard as he could.

Lefty let out a mighty yelp and jumped clear out of the sling on Mo's chest.

For a second she hung, suspended, in the air.

Then the cat landed, right on the middle of the old woman's sizable and sloping chest, and began scrabbling desperately to hang on.

Both the old woman and Mo released Will immediately.

The old woman let out a shriek that even Liesl, who had already left the train station and was winding her way through the dark and littered streets of Cloverstown, could hear.

"Get this beast—*ACHOO!*—off me!" she was screaming, as she danced around frantically, trying to use her cane to pry the cat from her chest. The harder she writhed and the more she twisted and turned, the harder Lefty clung to her chest. "Get the little monster—*ACHOO!*—off! It's clawing me!"

"Just stay still, won't you! I can't get 'er if you aren't still!" Mo was saying. "If you'd only stop *moving* for a second."

The policeman stood there dumbly, scratching his head.

And once again, Will ran.

"Hey," the policeman said glumly, watching the small boy dart into the crowd. "Hey. The boy is getting away."

But neither Mo nor the old woman paid him any attention. She was shrieking and dancing; Mo was trying to reason with her; Lefty had just started to bite at one of her earrings.

So the policeman shrugged, yawned, and went off in search of a nice potato doughnut. It had, after all, been a very long night.

EIGHTEEN

FOR SEVERAL HOURS, WILL WANDERED THE winding streets of Cloverstown aimlessly. He did not know whether he should be looking for the girl in the attic or not. It was possible that the old woman was correct: Perhaps she was off her rocker. But the idea was distressing to him, and Will did not want to believe it. Still, she *had* run from him. And the look on her face! The horror and fear! It made Will sick to think of it.

Then there was the fact of her appearance in Cloverstown at all. What, Will wondered, could she possibly be doing here? He hoped she had not been sent away to be a factory girl. Even more terrible than the memory of the horror on her face when she had seen him was the idea of that sweet, pale face bent over a sewing machine or a whirling cauldron of chemicals, those long, elegant fingers picked to bits by needles or scalded with hot liquids. He felt if she had been sent away to work, he must rescue her.

And so he walked, both looking and not looking, hopeful and fearful, and slowly moved farther and farther away from the train station, into the heart of the city, and then even farther, into its outskirts.

Eventually he came to an area that was very bad. All the buildings were rammed so close together it looked as though they were hugging for warmth, and the trash was piled in great heaps on either side of the narrow streets, which were full of beggars of all ages—old beggars, young beggars, blind beggars, lame beggars. The smells of people and waste were overwhelming. Will felt as though he would choke.

From all sides people pressed around him, pawing his jacket, touching his hair, murmuring, "Just a coin, just a coin, lad," and "Have a heart, spare a little."

"I'm sorry," Will said. He had never seen such a sea of ragged and sad-looking people, walking bones, shadow-lives. It made his heart ache. "I have no money myself." He hurried on, and silently said a prayer that the girl from the attic had not come this way.

He wondered if he should not, after all, return to the train station and continue north, as he had originally intended. But the idea of the girl tugged him on, just as she had drawn him back to that same street corner under her window, again and again, for months.

Then he left the people behind and came to an area at the far, far edges of Cloverstown. The buildings were long, low warehouses, and carts piled with goods came in and out, drawn by sad-looking animals whose ribs were showing. The air was so black and thick with grime that Will could taste it. Many of the warehouses were shuttered. In others, Will could make out thin, sad faces wavering behind cracked and dirt-encrusted windows, like pale flames. In others, service doors had been flung open to admit the carts and the animals, and Will could see men moving slowly in the vast, gloomy inner spaces.

He had, constantly, the prickly feeling of being watched, and he began to feel afraid without knowing exactly why. The warehouses became farther and farther apart, separated by long stretches of broken cobblestone and interspersed brown grasses. For a long time he passed no one. But still he felt eyes on him, and anxiety began to grow in the pit of his stomach—a gnawing, desperate feeling. It was not helped by the fact that his last meal had been the potato, nearly twenty-four hours earlier.

Will made a sudden resolution. He would ask the next person he came across for directions back to the train station. Then he would get on a train going north and forget all about the girl from the attic.

At that moment he was walking alongside an enormous building, built of black and moldering stone, and coated with white ash. It would have appeared to be abandoned, but for the black smoke churning from its four black chimneys. He thought he could detect the low murmur of conversation; and coming around the corner, he saw two men— both with filthy, knotted hair, and dirt-coated hands, and black and rotted teeth—standing in between several tarp-covered carts. Will could not see what the carts were holding. From the rectangular shapes outlined under the tarps, he thought boxes of some kind.

The men were deep in conversation, and arguing about something. Will did not like to interrupt them—they did not look particularly friendly—but he sucked in a deep breath and screwed up his courage and went closer.

As he approached, he could hear them better.

One of them was in the middle of jabbing his gnarled pointer finger into the middle of the other one's chest.

"I told you them round-saws was dangerous," he was saying. "That's the fourth boy what's lost his arm messing around with one of those things, and it's only been a month."

The other man picked his teeth, unconcerned. "Hazards of the trade," he drawled. "Saws is needed to cut wood. Wood is needed to make coffins."

"Don't tell me how to run my work," the first one growled. "The problem is the boys. We're running through 'em! We're running out! Boys is losing limbs, fingers, toes. One of the boys had his head chopped off last month!"

"I can find you boys," the second one said. "It shouldn't be a problem to find you a boy."

Will stopped, half-hidden behind a cart. He stood very, very still. His heart was beating loudly, and he willed it to be quiet.

"You better find me a boy!" cried the first one. "And right away, too, or it's you what's have to pay for the work I'm losing!"

Will began to back away, very carefully, from the two men, going as quickly as possible while still moving silently. He had no desire now to speak up—no desire at all. He was quite fond of his fingers, toes, limbs, *and* head; he did not particularly like the idea of losing them to a saw.

And then he stepped on a bit of broken glass. The glass went *CRUNCH!* very loudly under his boots.

Both men whipped their heads in his direction. Will dropped to a crouch behind one of the larger carts. This one was already hooked up to a donkey. The donkey sat, sadly pawing the dirt and nibbling at a single piece of frozen black grass.

"What was that?" growled the first man.

"Seems like we got ourselves a little spy," said the second, and Will could *hear* him grinning. "Maybe a little boy, like? Wouldn't *that* be nice? Suit yer needs just fine and dandy."

The men began clomping heavily in Will's direction. Any second now, they would see him, and Will would be dragged off to some factory, to be beaten and mistreated and probably told he was useless, just as he had been at the alchemist's. In desperation, Will swung himself onto the cart, lifted the heavy canvas tarp that was covering its load, and slipped underneath, at precisely the moment the men once again came into view.

Underneath the tarp it was dark and warm. Will closed his eyes, lay very still, and prayed.

For a moment there was the sound of shuffling boots,

and some confused murmurs. Then the first man said, "Well, I'll be dagged. I coulda swore I heard somethin'."

"Probably a rat."

"Don't be stupid. A rat's got no footsteps."

"I've seen rats in your factory so big, it's a miracle they don't got boots and a pocket watch."

"Oh, yeah . . . ? At least my wife don't put rats in the stew when meat's running low. . . ."

"That's cuz you don't got a wife. . . ."

The men's voices grew more remote. Will allowed himself a small sigh of relief. They were walking away. When he could no longer hear them, he opened his eyes.

And found himself staring at the girl from the attic.

He started to cry out, but she brought a finger quickly to her lips and shook her head, and he swallowed back the sound.

At that moment, the cart gave a tremendous, lurching movement forward, and Will heard someone saying, "Whoa, girl, whoa. Give me a second, give me a second. We'll be on our way in no time." Will assumed this was the driver, speaking to the donkey, and he was right. Boots scraped up at the front of the carriage; a leather whip slapped against the side of the cart; the man said, "Okay, thatta girl, nice and easy"; and the cart began lurching noisily forward.

Finally Will thought it safe to speak. "What—what—what are you doing here?"

"Stowing away," the girl said placidly. "What does it look like I'm doing?"

"Stowaways are on boats," Will couldn't help but point out.

"Well, hitching a ride, then. We need to go west. This cart is going west. I heard the men saying so. So we got in."

Will was not sure whether the girl from the attic had recognized him or not. She showed no signs of being inclined to run away. Of course, perhaps that was because she was trapped underneath a tarp, on a moving cart, surrounded by . . . Will squinted, trying to make out the wooden forms all around him, jostling in the darkness. His stomach squirmed. Coffins. They were surrounded by wooden coffins. Will hoped they were empty.

The girl-no-longer-in-the-attic was sitting in a narrow space between coffins, holding the box on her lap. It looked, Will thought, awfully like the kind of box the alchemist had used to transport magic, but he put the thought out of his mind. He would not think about the alchemist again, now or ever.

He lowered himself into the narrow space next to her. The girl's eyes appeared to flit briefly to the empty air immediately to his left, and she stifled a giggle.

"What's so funny?" he asked.

"Nothing." She bit her lip. "You nearly squashed them, that's all. But I don't suppose they can be squashed, really, so it's all right."

Will was confused. They were all alone in the cart; unless the coffins really were full of dead people, an idea that made him sick just to think of. "Squashed who?"

She opened her mouth, seemed about to say something, but instead just shook her head.

Perhaps it was as the woman with the cane said: Perhaps the girl really was mad as a hatter. He did not know whether the idea made him nervous or just sad. "Why did you run away from me before?" he asked, as a test.

The girl squinted at him for a second. Briefly, a look of alarm passed over her face. "You're the boy I saw at the train station," she said, recognizing him for the first time. "You were with the policeman and the old woman."

"I wasn't *with* them," Will said irritably.

"Well, *I* thought you were," the girl said. "That's why I ran. They tried to have me arrested." She squinted at him again and said suspiciously, "If you're not with the police, then how come you're following me?"

"I'm not following you," Will said, and then in his head added, *not exactly*. He thought the girl seemed sane enough, even if she did have imaginary friends, and decided to be honest. "I'm a runaway," he said. "I've got nowhere to go."

The girl's face lit up. "We're runaways too! We've got no home at all anymore. Well, I suppose they've never really had a home—not for the longest time, anyway. I wouldn't say the Other Side counts."

"The Other Side?" Will was confused again. "What are you talking about? And who's 'they'?"

The girl bit her lip. She seemed to regret having spoken. "They," she said. "Po and Bundle. Can't you see them?"

Will had just about decided that the girl was definitely crazy when at the very edges of his vision he saw something flicker. He sat very still and focused on the dark. There was something moving there, just barely, a shape slowly asserting itself in the darkness, as though the air was water and something—no, two things—were moving underneath its surface. And then, all at once, he could see them: a child-shaped bit of shadow, or air, roughly his size, and another small, fuzzy thing that looked at first glance to be a dog. Or maybe a cat. Difficult to say: Its outlines were not particularly clear.

Will let out a sharp gasp. "What—what are they?"

"What do we look like?" The voice was sharp and irritable.

The girl pointed. "That's Po," she said. "You'll have to forgive its manners. No one has any on the Other Side. And that's Bundle."

The shaggy thing made a noise somewhere between a bark and a meow.

Will gulped. "But they're—are they—are they really ghosts?"

"You can speak to me directly," Po said peevishly, and its outlines got a little brighter, as though they were catching fire. "I'm right here."

The girl said, "Of course they're ghosts. What else would they be?"

"But are they—are you—are they—" He felt foolish for stammering, and even more foolish for the question he was about to ask, but he couldn't help it. He did not know whether to speak to Po or the girl, so he just closed his eyes and quickly blurted out, "Aren't ghosts dangerous? I mean, don't they hurt people?"

"If you don't stop asking idiotic questions," Po said, "I'll give you a case of the shivers that'll have your teeth dancing a jig."

"Po," the girl said reproachfully. "Be nice."

Po became all at once a solid, squat mass of black. Will could only assume the ghost was sulking.

"They're not at all dangerous," the girl said, turning to Will. "Bundle's quite friendly."

As if to prove it, at that moment Will felt a softening around him. He looked down in his lap and saw a pair of coal-black, eye-shaped shadows blinking up at him. Bundle went, *Mwark*. Will lifted his hand tentatively and stroked the air where it was, for lack of a better word, different— more drape-y and shape-y.

"See?" The girl nodded her approval. "And Po is wonderful—when it's not being a grouch," she added a little louder, and Po muttered something Will could not make out.

He had noticed, however, that the girl called Po "it," and he wondered about that. "Isn't Po a boy or a girl?"

"Neither. And both. Those things lose meaning on the Other Side. Just like Bundle is both a dog and a cat, and also neither."

Will found it all very strange. "But they must have been one or the other at some time. When they were, um, on this side?"

"Oh, yes, I suppose so." The girl seemed unconcerned. "But they can hardly be expected to remember. They've been on the Other Side for a very long time. So now they are just Bundle and Po, and my friends." She leaned closer. "They helped me run away from the attic. That's where I'd been living."

At the mention of the attic, Will's heart jumped a little. He thought of saying, *I know*, and telling her how he used to stand on the street corner and watch her, but was too shy to do so. Instead he asked, "Why did you run away?"

The girl squirmed and appeared, for the first time,

uncomfortable. "It was time," she said vaguely, her hand skating over the wooden box in her lap. Will wondered what it contained. He thought, too, of the wooden box he was supposed to have delivered to the Lady Premiere, the one that had started all his troubles: It had looked very much like Liesl's box. No doubt it was being used by Mr. Gray for some disgusting purpose, for storing frogs' legs or newt eyeballs or something. "What about you?" she asked. "What's your story?"

Will did not want to appear incompetent by telling her about the mix-up with the alchemist's magic, so instead he said, "Oh, I just wanted to explore a bit. Get off to see the world, and so on."

In the corner, Po coughed. Will wondered if the ghost could somehow tell he was lying. He pressed on quickly, "I headed to the train station and jumped on the first train I could find. Hid out in the bathroom while the ticket collector came along, so I wouldn't get in trouble for riding without a ticket."

"That was very clever of you," the girl said, and Will glowed with pleasure. As far as he knew, no one had ever thought him clever before. "We had to hide out with the luggage. It was very dusty."

"Yes, well, I've done it loads of times," Will said again,

with a bit of swagger. He was enjoying the girl's attention. "I'm always on the move."

Po coughed again.

The girl, at least, seemed to believe him. Her eyes grew wide. "Don't your parents miss you?"

Now it was Will's turn to squirm. "I don't—er—I don't have any parents. I'm an orphan."

"I'm sorry," the girl said. She was quiet for a moment. "I'm an orphan too. Both of my parents are dead."

"Oh," Will said. "I'm sorry."

"My father is on the Other Side now," the girl said. "That's why we're heading west. So we can bring his ashes back to the willow tree, and he can rest, and go Beyond." She gestured to the box in her lap.

"I see," Will said, even though he didn't, exactly. The girl was weirder than he'd imagined she would be. But he wasn't sure he minded.

"Perhaps your parents are on the Other Side too."

"Perhaps," Will said doubtfully. He had never given it much thought. They had died when he was only a newborn, during an influenza outbreak, and he had no memories of them.

Suddenly the girl began to laugh. "Two homeless orphans," she said, "and two ghosts. We make a funny team, don't we?"

Will said, "I guess so."

Po grumbled, "Some team."

Bundle went, *Mwark*.

The girl put out her small, pale hand. "I'm Liesl," she said.

Will's heart gave another jump. Liesl. All this time he had desperately wanted to know her name, and there it was, and as soon as he knew it, he saw it fitted her exactly. "I'm William," he said. "But you can call me Will."

He took her hand, and they smiled at each other across the dark, as the cart carrying coffins and four stowaways rattled west.

PART III

REVERSALS & REUNIONS

NINETEEN

IT HAD BEEN A VERY DIFFICULT YEAR FOR MRS.
Snout, owner of Snout's Inn and Restaurant, which stood
on Crooked Street in Gainsville. Gainsville was the last
populated town for forty-seven miles: After Gainsville,
the road wound up through the ruddy hills, and then down
again, and all around there was nothing but fields and fields
and the occasional farmhouse.

For this reason, Snout's Inn and Restaurant had never
been particularly successful. There simply weren't enough
travelers on the road: only the occasional trapper headed
north, or vagrant farmhands looking for work. Still, if
a traveler did come to Gainsville, he or she was bound to
stop at Snout's Inn, as there was simply nowhere else to go.
And so Mrs. Snout had watered down her stews, and rarely

changed the linens, and hired for an assistant a small, rather dull boy who had lost an eye in a mining accident, and wildly underpaid him, and fed her guests scraps of feet and brain instead of nice cuts of meat without their knowledge, and so she had always squeaked by.

But this year had been hard—very, very hard.

That was why she had consented to take on the black-haired man who had shown up on her doorstep earlier in the day, growling that he needed a room and a meal, even though she could tell that he was as crooked as the street the inn was standing on—a robber, no question, and perhaps a murderer, too. But he had offered her two solid silver pieces—very dirty pieces of silver, and no doubt stolen, but money was money—and she had been unable to refuse.

Now she watched him greedily slurping up his third bowl of potato soup, whitish liquid dribbling appallingly down his long and filthy beard, and sighed to herself. There had been a time—long ago, it seemed, when the sun had still shone—when the farms had flourished, and she had hosted at her table good, honest workers, plowmen and reapers and apple pickers and cattle ranchers, and they had drunk her weak wine, and overpaid for it gladly, and laughed long and loud and stayed up to sing songs and tell stories around the fire.

When she heard a soft but insistent knocking at her front

door, for a moment she had a wild fantasy that she would open her door to find a whole group of red-faced, smiling men, who would greet her with a great "Hullo, there!" and fill the house with noise and laughter.

She was therefore highly disappointed when she opened the door and saw only a small, shivering girl and a very thin boy with extremely large, and very pink, ears. It had started to rain. Both of the children were soaking wet.

"Excuse me," the boy said, and Mrs. Snout saw at once he was trying to act brave for the girl's sake. "We were hoping we might have a room for the night."

"We've come a long way," the girl said. Her voice was soft and gentle. "And we're very tired." And Mrs. Snout saw that she was. The girl's eyelids kept fluttering as though desperate to close.

"Rooms are a dollar and twenty pence a night," Mrs. Snout said.

The children exchanged a glance. "We—we have no money," the boy said, his voice faltering.

"Then I have no rooms," Mrs. Snout replied, and began to shut the door.

"Please!" the girl piped up. "Please, we can work. We'll do dishes, or the sweeping."

Mrs. Snout peered closely at them. The little girl was

wearing a coat that, although worn and threadbare in places, looked as though it might once have been expensive, and she was carrying a large, polished wooden box. Outside, it was gray and gloomy and dark. The streets were very still. "How did you get here?" Mrs. Snout asked suspiciously. "And where are you coming from?"

Again, the small, pale children exchanged glances. Mrs. Snout could not put her finger on it—no, she couldn't say for certain—but she almost had the impression that both of them paused momentarily, as though listening to the wind.

And indeed, both Will and Liesl had been waiting while Po said, "I don't see the harm in telling her."

"We came from Cloverstown," the boy said after a moment. "We came by, um, coach."

"Then you must have some money," Mrs. Snout said. "Coaches aren't free."

"We—we used it up," the boy stuttered. He seemed to be growing desperate.

Mrs. Snout nodded to the box in the girl's arms. "And what's that, eh? You won't pretend you're carting around an empty jewelry box. What do you have? Out with it." Behind her, something clattered to the floor: The black-haired man had dropped his spoon.

The girl clutched the box tightly to her chest. "Nothing!" she said emphatically. "There is nothing at all inside."

"I cannot help you if you will not be honest with me." Mrs. Snout again started to close the door.

"Please!" Will stuck his foot in the door just as Mrs. Snout was swinging it shut, to prevent it from closing all the way. He was exhausted and freezing; his clothes were damp; the long and bumpy ride in the cart had left his legs numb. "We'll stay only one night. In the morning we head west, beyond the hills."

"Maybe you know it," Liesl put in eagerly. "We're going to the Red House."

The door, which was open only a small crack, barely enough to admit Will's foot, swung open a little wider. Mrs. Snout's mood shifted.

"The Red House, hmmm?" She looked Will and Liesl over more closely, and seemed to come to a decision. "Wait here."

Then she disappeared into the house. Liesl got a quick view of an ugly, black-haired man staring intently at her from a room farther into the house before the door clicked shut in her face.

They waited. Po asked, "What's taking her so long?"

and flitted about impatiently, but neither Liesl nor Will had the energy to answer.

Then Mrs. Snout was back. She was carrying two hot potatoes wrapped in a tea towel.

"Here," she said, passing the potatoes to Will, who felt tears of gratitude spring to his eyes. He had to blink them away quickly, so Liesl would not see. "I can't let you have a room if you've got no money to pay. But the barn around back will be warm and dry. You can sleep there tonight."

"Thank you," Liesl said fervently. The smell of the potato made her stomach growl.

"Mmmm," Mrs. Snout grunted. Again she watched them closely, through narrow eyes. "The walk to the Red House is long. Do you know the way?"

"I—I think I'll remember," Liesl said. Will thought she sounded uncertain.

"You will come to a green house after you've climbed the foothills," Mrs. Snout said. "That is Evergreen Manor. You must stop there. Tell Mrs. Evergreen I sent you. She will give you food and water and point you in the right direction."

Liesl would have hugged Mrs. Snout, except that Mrs. Snout did not seem like the kind of person who liked to be hugged. So instead she just said, "Thank you," once again.

"Mmmm." Mrs. Snout jerked her chin in the direction of the barn. "Now go on with you. It's late and you should be sleeping." And with that she shut the door again. This time Will and Liesl heard the latch sliding into place.

The black-haired man was not in the dining room when Mrs. Snout returned to it. He had left his bowl sitting in a small pool of spilled soup. She shook her head. No manners. Well, at least he had gone to bed. It made her distinctly uncomfortable to have him hanging around. His very presence gave her an itchy, evaluated feeling, as though every time he looked at her he was only trying to determine how much he could get for prying out her fillings and selling them, or chopping her body into neat cuts of meat for the butcher.

Mrs. Snout passed into the kitchen, where her half-blind assistant was squatting in the corner playing with a ball of string, like a cat.

"You," Mrs. Snout said, and the boy scrambled to his feet. One eye blinked guiltily at her. The other was a mere hole, a bit of scratched skin. Mrs. Snout never got used to looking at it. Instead she focused on the tip of his nose.

"You are to take Benny"—that was the mule, a skinny, bad-tempered thing—"and ride at once to Evergreen Manor."

"Yes'm."

She fished the trim white card from her apron pocket. It had been given her in the morning by a woman with a long fur coat. The script across its front was elegant, and it smelled vaguely of expensive perfume. She checked the name on the card briefly. "You are to find the Lady Premiere and tell her we have news of the runaway children. Tell her that they are on their way to the Red House. Say it back to me."

"They are on their way to the Red House," the boy repeated dutifully.

Mrs. Snout nodded. "They should reach Evergreen by tomorrow evening. Tell the Lady Premiere to be prepared."

"Yes'm." The boy mashed his hat on his head determinedly and prepared to set off.

"Not so fast!" Mrs. Snout glared fixedly at his nose. "This is most important. You must demand the reward she offered. Two whole gold pieces, and no less. Do not return without the money."

Mrs. Snout sighed as the boy scrambled out the back door. She passed her fingers once more along the little white card, then slipped it back into her apron.

Desperate times, she thought, called for desperate measures.

TWENTY

LIESL AND WILL ATE THEIR POTATOES GREEDILY
even before they reached the old barn—so quickly they
barely tasted them, and burned their tongues and fingers in
the process. The potatoes made only the tiniest, barest dent
in their hunger, but they were better than nothing.

In the corner of the barn—which was, as the innkeeper
had said, dry and relatively warm, and which smelled only
the very smallest bit like animal droppings—they found a
single wool blanket.

"We'll have to share," Liesl said, yawning, and placed
the wooden box carefully on the floor. Then she and Will
lay down beside it and pulled the blanket up to their chins.
"You'll keep watch, won't you, Po?" she said drowsily.

"Yes," Po said. "I'll wake you at dawn."

Neither Will nor Liesl said thank you. Under the blanket, both of their small chests rose in unison, like swells in the ocean, and after only a minute the barn was filled with the quiet sounds of snoring.

Po, watching them, felt a twinge, as though a large hand had reached out and pinched its Essence. The ghost was startled and bothered by the feeling. Distant memories tugged at Po: a ring of children, chanting something (*game*, the word appeared to Po suddenly), and Po standing on the outside, left out.

Left out: two more words the ghost had not thought of for the longest of long times. What did belonging mean to a ghost? What did it matter? A ghost belonged to nothing but the Other Side, and the air, and the deep, dark tunnel of time that has no walls or ceiling or floor, but only goes on forever.

We've been too long on the Living Side, Po thought to Bundle, and as usual Bundle *mwark*ed his approval. "We don't belong here."

Mwark.

"Come on. We must go back to our place and get away for a bit." And Po felt the living world—with all its corners and boundaries and hard, sharp edges—disappearing as it crossed back into the Other Side.

Po only intended to stay away a minute or two. No harm would come to Liesl, the ghost was sure of it.

But time is not easy to measure on the Other Side, where infinity is the only boundary, and seconds do not exist, nor minutes nor hours nor years: only space and distance. And so on the Living Side, Liesl and Will slept soundly, and minutes added up to an hour, and just after midnight the door creaked open and the black-haired man slipped silently into the barn.

He was, as Mrs. Snout had guessed, a career criminal. His nickname was Sticky, and he was a thief. He would steal anything that wasn't nailed down: money from church collection plates, candy from a baby, the shirt off the back of a beggar. The reputation of his long, pale fingers, which attracted wallets, coins, and earrings like a magnet attracts steel filings, had earned him his nickname.

He had seen the little girl clutching the wooden box protectively to her chest and, like Mrs. Snout, suspected she was lying when she had claimed there was nothing inside.

Why would she be carrying an empty box with her?

And not just any box, Sticky thought: a jewelry box. Standing in the dark, listening to the two children snoring, he allowed himself a small smile of satisfaction, imagining the beautiful jewels he would find winking in its rich velvet interior, the gold and silver, the tiny flashing stones.

It would be, he fantasized, the payload he had been waiting for his whole life, since he had lain in his narrow cot as a young boy in Howard's Glen, next to his pushy and pinchy older sister, and dreamed of someday having money to buy an enormous house of his own, and money to bathe in, and money to roll between his fingers. Money to burn and waste and hoard and love!

He moved silently across the barn. Not even the bats, sleeping in the rafters, were disturbed by his progress. As always, his heart was beating rapidly— not from nerves, because he had years of practice and was excellent at what he did—but from pleasure and excitement.

Closer, closer, closer. Finally he stood just beside the two slumbering forms, each folded like twin commas. Slowly—moving inch by inch now—he knelt to the ground and removed from his overcoat the small rectangular wooden box he had stolen from Mrs. Snout's pantry, which contained a load of potato flour. He allowed himself another small smile. It was, as he expected, almost exactly the same dimensions as the girl's box, and roughly the same weight, which meant that with any luck he would be miles and miles away before she noticed the substitution.

He tucked the jewelry box carefully under his arm and left the box filled with flour in its place, barely concealing a chuckle of glee. It was really so easy . . . almost *too* easy. . . .

Then Sticky slipped back across the barn and out into the night. Liesl slept; Will slept; the bats slept. Everyone slept, it seemed, but for the black-haired thief who moved through the streets of Gainsville quickly and with purpose, carrying (though he did not know it, of course) the greatest magic in all the world.

Some time later, Po and Bundle squeezed through a narrow opening in the folds between worlds and re-entered the Living Side. Po was surprised to find that outside, the edges of the sky were lightening. They had been gone for longer than the ghost had anticipated.

At that moment, Liesl stirred. She sat up, rubbing her eyes and blinking.

"Is it time to get up?" she asked, her voice still thick with sleep. Next to her, Will groaned.

"Yes," Po said.

Liesl yawned broadly. "Poor Po," she said. "You must get so bored, just sitting there watching us all night."

Po felt another foreign twinge (*guilt* was the word, only recovered that instant). "It's not too bad," the ghost said vaguely.

"Po can't sit down, anyway," Will said, raising himself onto both elbows. His hair was sticking up most ridiculously. "Can you, Po? You don't have legs to fold or a bottom to sit on."

Po did not dignify Will's comment with a response. Instead it just flitted to the window and said, "We should go."

Po had debated telling Liesl it had gone to the Other Side, but Will's comment made the ghost decide firmly against it.

Besides, Po thought, the box was clearly sitting right next to her, and no harm had been done.

In its mind, Bundle went, *Mwark.*

TWENTY-ONE

THE WAY OUT OF GAINSVILLE WAS BARE AND
bleak, though it must once have been less so. On either side
of the narrow dirt road, bald brown fields extended toward
the horizon. Most of the farms had been abandoned years
ago, and nothing looked familiar to Liesl.

The rain, at least, had stopped, and it was slightly warmer
than it had been for some time, so both Liesl and Will were
able to unbutton their coats. Still, it was slow going, especially when the road began to wind up into the foothills.
Here the path became less clear. For long stretches it disappeared altogether, and Bundle and Po had to float on ahead
and come back and report the correct way, so that Liesl and
Will would not exhaust themselves tracing and retracing
their steps.

Everyone's temper ran short.

"I swear," Liesl said for the hundredth time, pausing to wipe sweat off her brow, "this box is heavier than it was yesterday."

"If you would let me carry it . . . ," Will said, also for the hundredth time.

"No!" Liesl said sharply.

Will muttered something under his breath and went on ahead.

"What did you say?" Liesl's heart was beating very fast.

"I said it's loony!" Will cried out, turning back to her. "This whole trip is loony!" And then, frustrated, he kicked a very large stone to his left. Pain shot through his toes and he began hopping up and down. "We've been walking all day and we're not getting anywhere. I've passed this rock twenty times in the past two hours, I'd swear to it!"

"Are you questioning my capacity to navigate?" Po asked coldly, and Bundle made a noise somewhere between a growl and a hiss.

"I'm sorry if I'm not particularly inclined to believe a ghost. Probably just bringing us out here to kill us."

"So I could spend eternity in your delightful company? I don't think so."

"Stop it, stop it, stop it!" Liesl cried out, so loudly that Will and Po did, in fact, stop it. She sank to the ground. "It's no use," she said. "We'll never make it. We don't know where we are; we don't know the way. And you two are fighting. It's horrible. I can't stand it." A tear slid down her cheek to the very tip of her chin.

Will forced a laugh. "Me and Po weren't fighting. We were just, um, joking around. Weren't we, Po?"

"What is joking?" Po asked, but seeing the way Will glared, quickly said, "Oh, yes. Yes. Joking."

Liesl wiped her nose on the cuff of her jacket. "Really?" She sniffed.

Will nodded vigorously, and the ghost flickered its agreement. Both were desperately uncomfortable, and unhappy because Liesl was unhappy. Above all, they wished—fervently, more than anything—that a second tear would not follow the first, as neither had any experience with a crying girl.

Only Bundle went to her and wrapped its Essence as close to hers as possible, so that in her soul she felt a comforting warmth. She wiped the tear from her chin with her forearm.

Will felt encouraged to speak again. "Er—it'll be all

right, Liesl," he said, feeling horribly awkward. "We'll get there. You'll see."

Just then a terrible, shrill scream echoed up through the hills. Liesl gasped and nearly dropped the wooden box. Will jumped, and even Po flashed momentarily to the Other Side, reappearing a second later.

"What was that?" Liesl asked. Instantly she forgot about the difficult way ahead, and the fact that Po and Will had been fighting.

"Sounded like a wolf or something," Will said uncertainly. He had never actually heard a wolf, but he imagined they would howl like that.

"We must move on," Po said. "It will be dark soon."

Liesl climbed heavily to her feet. Every one of her muscles ached. And this time, when Will reached out and said, "Here, let me," she passed him the box.

"Don't drop it," she said.

"Never."

"Swear?"

He made an X over his heart.

They walked on.

TWENTY-TWO

THE TERRIBLE SCREAM THAT HAD SO STARTLED
Liesl and her friends did not come from a wolf.

It came from Sticky, who had at that moment—having
finally reached an area he felt was sufficiently remote—
lowered the wooden box to the ground with eager, trembling
fingers, and unlatched it.

How to describe his fury—his outrage—his pure and
searing disappointment—when instead of piles of rubies
and strands of pearls and little, clinking rings—he had
instead beheld a pile of dust, of nothing, of worthlessness?
(For so the magic looked to him—like dust.)

There is no way to describe his feelings at that moment.
Even *he* could not describe them, which was why, instead,
he screamed: a great, long howl, which carried up all the
way into the hills.

Had Sticky taken the time to examine the contents of the box more closely, he might have noticed some interesting and unusual features of the substance that, at first glance, appeared to be dust. He might have noticed the very slight way it shimmered, almost as if it was moving and shifting ever so slightly. He might have noticed, too, that from certain angles it appeared to *shine*, just like the long-missing sun, and that it was not a uniform dark gray color, but a hundred different colors all at once—blue and purple and red and green.

But he did not look more closely. Enraged, he drew his leg back and gave the box a quick, hard kick. The box flew several feet and landed heavily with a large crack. Sticky noticed with satisfaction that the latch had broken off and the box had sprung open.

Then something occurred to him: The girl had made a fool of him. She had known, somehow, that he was after the jewelry, and so had replaced it with a box full of dust before sleeping. Yes, yes; it must be so. She believed she could outwit him.

The idea was like a deliverance. The jewelry existed—it *must* exist. The future that Sticky had dreamed of for himself all those years ago was still within reach. (And *how* he would take revenge on that snipe-y, snoopy sister of his once he was rich! He would track her down, wherever she was, and make her pay for every time she had pulled his ears, and pinched his elbows, and called him a worm!)

Sticky remembered that the girl had asked the way to the Red House, and so he set off in that direction. This time, there would be no midnight sneaking. This time, he would have the girl's riches, even if he had to pry them from her cold, dead fingers.

Sticky smiled.

The magic—now exposed to the air—spilled from the box onto the ground. Slowly, very slowly, encouraged by the wind, it began skipping and spreading over the surface of the world.

TWENTY-THREE

EVENTUALLY THE IMPERFECT PATH THAT LIESL, Will, Po, and Bundle followed began to wind down and out of the hills. The stars were smoldering behind a thin covering of clouds by the time they were at last on flat ground. By then the path had disappeared. All around them were dark, bare fields; and in the distance, a house, with candles burning brightly in its windows.

"That must be Evergreen," Liesl said. "We'll rest there for the night."

Nobody argued. It had been a long, exhausting hike. Even Po was tired—not physically, of course, but from a deep ache in its Essence, from flitting ahead and doubling back all the time, and having to wait for the others to catch up, and keep itself from speaking out when *yet again* Will had to stop and shake a pebble from his too-large shoes.

It was very quiet and very still as they set off across the frost-coated ground toward the house. With every step, Liesl grew happier. Soon they would have soft beds to sleep in, and perhaps a meal. And they were close to the Red House now, she was sure of it—it was only a mile or two beyond the end of the hills. Tomorrow they would finish their journey, and her father's soul would be at rest. And then . . .

Well, the truth was, she was not sure what would happen then, but she pushed the thought out of her mind. Po would come up with something. Or she and Will would go to work at Snout's Inn, where the woman had been so kind.

Will, too, felt he could not get to Evergreen fast enough. The box was heavy—Liesl had not lied—and he was so hungry it was painful, as though there were a small animal scrabbling around in his stomach, sticking him with its claws.

When they were thirty feet from the house, Liesl got a last-minute burst of energy and broke into a run. "Come on, Will!" she called. "Almost there!"

Will tried to run and felt a sharp pain in his heel.

"Daggit." He had gotten another stone in his shoe. "Be there in a minute!"

Liesl had already reached the house and was knocking firmly on the door. Will sat down on a large rock, rolled up his pant leg, and wrestled his shoe from his foot, muttering curses as he did.

"Hello," he heard Liesl say as the front door opened. "We have come from Gainsville. Mrs. Snout said we might find lodging here."

Dimly, distantly, Will was aware of a large rectangle of light spilling out into the night, and the blurry, dark figure of a person silhouetted within it.

The silhouette crooned, "Of course, dearie, come in, come in!"

Panic shot through Will like a sudden jolt of electricity. All at once he forgot his exhaustion and the pebble in his shoe.

There was something wrong with the voice—something wrong with its sweetness.

It was *too* sweet, like flowers laid over a corpse.

He recognized it.

"Thank you," Liesl was saying, even as Will found his voice and screamed, "No, Liesl! No!"

Liesl turned, alarmed. But at that moment the Lady Premiere stepped out onto the porch and seized Liesl with both arms, snarling, as she did, "Come here, you nasty little creature!"

"Run, Will!" Liesl screamed as she was dragged backward into the house. "Don't stop until—"

He did not hear the rest of her sentence. The door swung shut, and there was nothing but silence.

TWENTY-FOUR

LIESL WOKE UP FEELING AS THOUGH SHE'D BEEN clubbed over the head—which, in fact, was almost exactly what *had* happened. During her frantic struggles against the Lady Premiere, she had smacked her head against the doorjamb and gone as limp as a lettuce leaf.

The Lady Premiere had thus made two important discoveries:

1. She much preferred children when they were unconscious.

2. The girl did not have the magic, which meant that the boy must have it.

Liesl was lying in a narrow bed in a plain white room. She was quite alone. She did not know what had happened to Bundle or Po, and she shivered a little underneath the thin wool blanket that was covering her.

From beyond the door she heard the muffled sounds of arguing: a man's voice she did not recognize, and the voice of the woman who had captured her.

"He can't have gotten far with it," the man was saying. "It's dark as pitch outside, and he's got nowhere to go."

"Then it should be easy for you to find him and bring him back!" the woman retorted. Liesl heard footsteps, and their voices receded, though she heard the man mutter "useless" several times.

Liesl looked around the room more closely. There was a small oil lamp burning in the corner, a plain wooden table next to the bed, and next to that, a chair. Otherwise the room was empty.

Liesl sat up slowly. As she did, the pain in her head intensified. For a moment she had to sit gripping the edge of the bed and repeating the word *ineffable* over and over.

At last she felt well enough to stand. She did not have to check the door to know that it was locked. Instead she went to the window. Her heart soared as it slid open effortlessly, then her heart immediately plummeted again. She was very high up—on the third or fourth floor, she thought, though it was hard to tell exactly—and the ground below her window was rocky and uneven. The nearest tree was twenty or thirty feet away—too far to reach, or jump to.

She was well and truly trapped, and could only hope Will was on his way to the Red House with the ashes.

She slid the window closed again, momentarily startled by her own image in the glass: Her face and the room behind her were reflected clearly against the backdrop of the darkness outside. She had so often seen herself this way, reflected in the attic window, as she stared out onto the world beyond the glass and fantasized about being a part of it. Now she *was* a part of it, and that girl—the caged girl in the window, stuck onto a pane of glass—seemed almost unrecognizable.

Things had changed. *She* had changed.

Liesl resolved that no matter what, she would escape. Even if she were all alone, even if it was hopeless, she would escape or die trying. Anything was preferable to being a prisoner again.

"Hello."

Liesl jumped as Po materialized suddenly beside her, followed closely by a very excited Bundle.

"Where did you go?" Though only moments earlier

Liesl had determined she would be okay on her own, the sight of her ghostly friends made her want to shout with joy.

"I went to tell Will what happened," Po said, "and to warn him that he is not safe."

"Is he okay? Did he escape? Is the box safe?" Liesl demanded eagerly.

"He is fine," Po said, sounding (to Liesl's mind) almost regretful. "He has made it to a stretch of woods, where he is quite concealed. The box is still in his possession."

"That's a relief," Liesl said. "Though how I'm going to get out of here is beyond—"

Just then, Bundle began *mwark*ing sharply.

"Shhh," Po hissed. "Someone is coming. Quick, in the bed."

Liesl leaped into the bed and pulled the covers to her chin, just as a key clicked neatly in the lock and her door swung inward.

"I see our little sleeping beauty has awoken," Augusta Hortense Varice-Morbower sang cheerfully, as she swept into the room, carrying a tray.

Liesl gasped. "What—what are you doing here?"

"Well, hello to you too, pumpkin." Augusta tried to smile but only managed to grimace.

"Who is that?" Po whispered.

"My stepmother," Liesl whispered back.

Augusta, who did not see Po, because she was used to seeing nothing but what could be bought, or weighed, or measured, thought that Liesl was only greeting her. "You know I've always despised that word," she said, setting the tray on the little table. On it was a bowl, covered with a dented metal lid.

"I won't call you mother," Liesl said, lifting her chin.

"Of course not, sugar pie. It's the *mother* part I object to most strongly." Augusta showed her teeth again.

It had been months since she had seen her stepmother, except from a distance. Augusta never came to the attic. Now Liesl was struck by how very ugly she was—even in her fine socks and expensive shoes and her silk dresses, she looked just like a toad, like a creature that should be wallowing in muck.

"How did you find me?" Liesl asked.

Augusta sat on the bed, which groaned under her substantial heft. "Well, you couldn't expect to get far, could you? Not pulling a stunt like that." She waggled a finger at Liesl. "The Lady Premiere is quite put out about the loss of her magic. Quite. The alchemist, too. It's all he could talk about on the carriage ride over—how he would torture the boy, when it was all over. Turn him into a worm and put him in a birdcage—things like that." Augusta said this with relish. She had decided she very much liked the alchemist. That was a man with a head on his shoulders!

Liesl felt hopelessly confused. "Magic . . . ?" she repeated. "I—I don't know what you're talking about."

Augusta stared at her narrowly. The girl appeared to be perfectly sincere. "Why did you run away?"

Liesl was quiet for a minute. Then she lifted her head. "I wanted to bring my father's ashes to the Red House, so he could rest. He told me to do it," she added, somewhat defensively. He hadn't exactly told her, of course, but he had told Po, and that was almost the same thing.

"Told you to, did he? You've talked to him, then?" Augusta asked, and there was a dangerous softness to her voice.

"Y-yes," Liesl said, after only a second's hesitation. "He wanted to be laid by the willow tree, near my mother." She did not feel like explaining about Po; it was obvious to her that her stepmother could not see either of the two ghosts.

Augusta's face hardened. She did not know what to believe. Either Liesl knew she had the magic and had raised the ghost of her father, or she did not know she had the magic and had not raised the ghost of her father. Either way, she was lying about something, and Augusta didn't like it. Not one small bit.

"You've seen him, then?" she asked, even more softly, and if Liesl had known her stepmother better, she would have known to be afraid.

"He is on the Other Side," Liesl answered in a roundabout way.

Augusta considered the little girl lying in the narrow bed. Perhaps she had underestimated Liesl, after all. *He wanted to be laid next to the willow tree, near my mother.* It did sound like something Henry Morbower would say, that floppy-hearted fool. Sickening. After all these years, he still had not forgotten that simple woman.

Augusta vowed then that whatever the truth, she would get rid of the ashes as soon as possible—preferably in some dark, dank hole. While Augusta was alive, Henry Morbower would never get to lie beside that useless flip of a first wife.

Then she composed her face into her best approximation of a smile, and lifted the lid off the bowl on the tray. Instantly, the room was filled with the delicious scent of rich butter and broth, carrots, and chicken. Liesl gaped. She had not seen food of such richness—and quantity—in ever so long, and her mouth began to water.

"Now, that's enough talk," Augusta said sweetly, leaning over to tuck a napkin in the collar of Liesl's shirt. "You've had a long, exhausting journey, and you must be starving. I want you to eat up." Her face was very close to Liesl's; her smile was a half-moon. "I want to be sure you are healthy and strong."

Augusta picked up the bowl with one hand and, with the other, filled a ladle-sized spoon to the brim with hot broth, and golden chicken, and rice, and carrots.

"Open wide," she crooned. "Here comes the airplane."

As much as Liesl resented being treated like a baby, she was too hungry to resist. She opened her mouth as the spoon came zooming toward her.

Then Po shouted suddenly, "No, Liesl! No! Don't eat it!"

She snapped her mouth shut quickly. The spoon collided with her chin and hot broth soaked into the napkin. The piece of chicken and the carrot rolled onto her lap.

"Stupid girl!" Augusta hissed, and then immediately recovered herself. "You must keep your mouth open, my dear."

Liesl was glaring at Po, who was standing next to the bed. Po's edges were flaring white with panic. "What'd you do that for?" she said.

"I didn't do anything," Augusta said, assuming that Liesl was addressing her. "I am just trying to make sure that my darling little dearest gets the soup Augusta made especially for her. Now, let's try that again, shall we?" She filled the spoon again.

Po was speaking in a rush. "Remember what your father said when I met him on the Other Side? He said, *I should never have eaten the soup.* Remember?"

Liesl's head was spinning. Images returned to her: peering down from the attic window, watching Augusta bustle out of the house on her way to the hospital, carrying a large tureen with both hands; lying next to the radiator and listening to the servants gossiping below her room, saying, "No matter what people say, the woman can't be all bad. She brings the master soup every single day, made by her own hands. Sits by his bed and feeds him too, won't let him waste a drop of it."

I should never have eaten the soup.

Terror and hatred crested suddenly inside of Liesl, and on its waves came a single word, clear and sharp and true.

Murder.

"Open wide!" Augusta said.

"No!" Liesl shouted, scrabbling backward on the bed, pressing up against the pillows, and striking out at the bowl with one foot. It flew off the bed and shattered against the wall, leaving a temporary tableau of limp parsley and liquid and onion bits on the plaster.

Augusta, enraged, sprang to her feet. She grabbed Liesl by the shoulders and shook her.

"Idiot!" she snapped. "Stupid, silly, terrible thing!"

Augusta shook Liesl so hard her teeth knocked together. But Liesl managed to cry out, "Murderer!"

Instantly Augusta released her. Liesl fell back on the sheets and then scrambled to her feet, placing the bed between herself and her stepmother.

"What did you say?" Augusta's voice had become quiet again, and this time Liesl could hear the danger there. But she didn't care. All the hatred filled her, fueled her, made her burn bright and hot and dangerous herself.

"Murderer," Liesl repeated. She squeezed her fists so tightly her nails dug into her palms.

Augusta stared at her for a moment. Her black eyes glittered like a snake's. "You don't know what you're saying," she said at last, coldly. "You've had a bad shock. You'll eat something, and then you'll sleep, and in the morning you'll feel better." Augusta stooped to collect the broken pieces of the soup tureen.

"I know exactly what I'm saying!" Liesl burst out. "You killed him. You poisoned him; and you lied to me; and you wouldn't let me see him as he was dying." Her voice trembled with fury.

For a moment, Augusta said nothing. Liesl thought she would deny it—a tiny piece of her almost *hoped* she would—but then Augusta smiled, and the smile was terrible, like the grin of a wild cat just before it pounces. Liesl felt a cold, sharp blade of terror knife through her. So it was true.

"Yes," Augusta said softly. "Yes, you've found me out. I killed him. Drop by drop, bit by bit, so no one would ever know. It was hard to be so patient. Very hard. But it was necessary." Her predator's grin grew slightly wider. "With you, my dear, I fear I will not be so indulgent. With you, I think it must go quickly."

"Stay away from me." Liesl could barely spit out the words. "I hate you."

Augusta regarded her stepdaughter critically for a minute, as though evaluating her. Then she said, "You know, I always thought you were quite stupid. It appears I underestimated you. But it is no matter now." She moved to the door. "I'll be back shortly, with a new bowl of soup. I made it especially for you, with extra butter. I promise you won't even taste the poison. I believe that people should enjoy their last meals, don't you?"

"I won't eat it!" Liesl cried. "You can't force me to!"

Augusta whirled around. "Then you will starve slowly," she hissed. "It is up to you how you choose to die, but you can count on this: Either way, you will not leave this house alive."

Then she spun out of the room and slammed the door shut behind her. Liesl heard the key turn sharply in the lock. Then footsteps, leaving. Then nothing.

TWENTY-FIVE

"THIS WOULD BE FAR EASIER IF YOU WERE A ghost," Po said for about the thousandth time.

"You've made that clear," Liesl said wearily.

"I'm only trying to help."

"I know, I know." Liesl rubbed her eyes. She had been up all night and was very tired. "I'm sorry."

"Are you sure you can't dematerialize? Not even a little?"

"I'm sure." Liesl sighed and sat down heavily on the bed. She had been pacing the tiny room for hours, from the bed to the locked door to the window, but the dimensions of her problem were always the same: She was trapped, with no possibility of escape. The second bowl of soup—poisoned, she was sure—was sitting cold and untouched on the bedside table, and Liesl knew what Augusta said was true. Eventually, she would either have to eat it or starve.

It was hopeless.

Po passed through the table and back, as though trying to show how easily it could be done. "*Far* easier if you were a ghost," it muttered.

Liesl stiffened. Then she stared at Po for so long that the ghost began to get nervous and faded to an almost imperceptible shadow-gray.

"Po," Liesl said, a note of wonder creeping into her voice. "You're absolutely right."

"I know I'm right," Po said, slightly uneasily, thinking that Liesl was behaving in very contradictory ways. One second she lectured; the next second she praised. Living ones were really quite incomprehensible. "But you aren't a ghost, are you? So it doesn't help us."

"No . . . ," Liesl said. A glimmer of a glimmer of an idea was taking shape in her mind. She struggled to hold on to it. "I'm not a ghost. But that doesn't mean I can't pretend to be one, for a little bit."

"I don't know what you're talking about," Po said. The ghost was starting to get irritated. It did not like riddles.

"I'm talking about *the Other Side*." Liesl sprang from the bed, eyes shining. "Don't you see? I can follow you there. I can cross. And then we'll cross back to the Living Side somewhere different—somewhere safe."

For a moment there was perfect silence. Liesl held her breath. Even Bundle was uncharacteristically still.

Then Po said, "Impossible."

"Why?" Liesl demanded. "Why is it impossible?"

"Living people cannot cross to the Other Side. It is unheard of. It can't be done."

"It *can't* be done or it *isn't* done?"

"Either. Both." Po was having trouble keeping its thoughts together. "It wouldn't work. It couldn't possibly work."

"When you go to the Other Side, you must slip back through some kind of opening, don't you?"

"Places where the universe is stretched thin, yes . . ."

"And you can choose where to cross back *from* the Other Side, can't you? You can find your way here through different tunnels and pathways?"

"Yes, within certain limits . . ."

"So why can't I do those things? Why can't you just lead me, in and out?" Liesl turned very serious. She lowered her voice. "Either way I'll end up on the Other Side, Po. If I don't find a way to get out of here, I'll be there soon enough."

Po was quiet again. The ghost had not thought of it that way.

Finally Po said, "I suppose I could try and . . . enlarge the opening somewhat. So that you could fit through with a body."

Liesl clapped her hands and bounced up and down excitedly. "I knew it! I knew we could do it."

"We don't know if we can do it at all," Po said sharply. "I said we could *try*. Once we're on the Other Side, you'll have to stick closely to me. It is vast, and some of its places are very strange."

"Okay," Liesl said, with a slight catch in her voice.

"I will lead you as quickly as I can to a different opening between the worlds, and we will cross back. I don't know what would happen to a living one who stayed too long on the Other Side. Nothing good, I imagine."

Liesl nodded. Her heart was beating very fast, and all of a sudden her throat felt desperately dry.

"Are you ready?" Po asked.

"Now?"

"I don't see any point in waiting," Po said. "Do you?"

Liesl shook her head. Her excitement had been replaced with fear. She regretted, now, having made the suggestion in the first place. But she knew, in her heart of hearts, that there was no other way.

"All right," Po said. "I will try to open a door for you." At the last second the ghost said, "I don't know how the Other Side will seem to you. It's possible you'll be frightened. It's probable you'll be confused. Perhaps it is better if you close your eyes. Follow the sound of my voice, and I will lead you through."

Liesl nodded. She squeezed her eyes shut tightly.

She thought she heard the smallest ripping sound, like a sheet of tissue paper being torn in two. Then she felt a cold wind on her face.

"Hurry," Po said, and Liesl could tell from the ghost's voice that it was straining. "Step forward."

Liesl stepped.

Suddenly all around her was howling, rushing confusion: the sensation of a thousand winds tearing at her from every side. The breath left her in an instant and she felt she was suffocating. She couldn't move; she couldn't breathe; her whole body felt like a scream.

And then she heard Po's voice, but somehow its voice was *inside* of her: like one part of her mind was speaking to the other part.

"Go quickly," the voice said. "Straight ahead. Don't open your eyes. Listen to me. Listen only to me."

Slowly, painfully, feeling as though she was moving through molasses, Liesl inched forward. The shrieking all around her grew worse; the wind tore at her skin and she felt her head would explode.

But she was aware of the sensation of Po inside of her, urging her forward: a comforting presence, but strange, too, like suddenly feeling a division down your middle and being two people. Bundle was there too, a wet and shaggy presence in her mind, all panting excitement and forward, forward, forward.

Liesl, carrying her ghostly friends inside of her Essence, walked the strange and twisted paths of the Other Side.

After what seemed like an eternity to Liesl—and was in fact both forever and the tiny, barest space between seconds at the same time, for those things have no meaning on the Other Side—Po spoke. Again its voice was strained.

"All right," it said. "It is safe to cross back now."

Liesl still had her eyes squeezed tightly shut. She was too scared to open them. She tried to move forward but hit a solid wall, directly in front of her.

"Come on!" Po urged her. "I cannot keep the door open forever."

"I can't!" Liesl cried out. "Something's blocking me."

"Nothing's blocking you. You have to trust me."

"I can feel it!" A sob was building in Liesl's throat. "There's a wall."

"Liesl." Po was speaking quietly, but she could feel the panic in its voice. "Liesl, the Other Side has started to take you. You are beginning to blur."

Liesl felt she would cry. Her body was filled with an impossible, heavy weight, as though she had been filled from head to toe with sand.

Po continued speaking. Its voice was shaking; it could not keep the space between sides open forever. "When I tell you to, you must jump. Okay? You must throw yourself forward."

"But—"

"No buts," Po said sharply. "Just do it."

"Okay," Liesl said, though she knew it was impossible. She could no longer move. She was frozen, paralyzed; she would be picked apart by winds like a dead animal by vultures.

Suddenly Po's voice was screaming in her mind. "Now, Liesl! Jump!"

Liesl willed her muscles to jump. She focused on the word with every single dark and dusty corner of her mind. She thought of the sparrows soaring off the roof of 31 Highland Avenue. She thought of air. She thought of her father.

And even though she moved only a tiny bit—just a mere fraction of an inch—it was enough. The bonds of the Other Side released her. She had the impression of an enormous tumble through space. She was in free fall; she wanted to scream. The shrieking winds around her reached a howling crescendo.

And then the winds and the shrieking stopped, and she was landing on her knees on damp, hard ground.

"You're safe," Po said. Its voice was outside of her again. "You can open your eyes."

They were standing at the edge of a dark forest. Evergreen Manor was several hundred feet behind them. Liesl could see the oil lamp burning in the room in which she had been confined, from this distance no more than a small square of pale light.

Po was barely visible. The ghost was exhausted from the effort of expanding the opening between sides of existence. It was a thin, bare outline in the dark.

"We did it." Liesl climbed to her feet. She was trembling a bit. She, too, was exhausted from her journey to the Other Side.

"Yes," Po said simply.

"Thank you."

"Yes," Po said.

It was strange to think that only a minute earlier she had been carrying the ghost inside of her. Liesl did not know whether to feel embarrassed or exhilarated or sad, so she felt everything at once. For the first time it struck her as a strange thing, to have such careful boundaries around the self, and to be your own person and only your own person, always when you were alive.

Then Liesl began to giggle. She did not know why, exactly, but all of a sudden it seemed to her absurd: A ghost had just saved her life by leading her through the land of the dead. Once she started giggling, she couldn't stop, and soon she had to double over and her stomach hurt from laughing.

"I don't see what's so funny," Po said. Its outlines began to reassert themselves more clearly.

"Oh, Po." Liesl wiped tears from the corner of her eyes and let out another bark of laughter. "You wouldn't."

Bundle went, *Mwark*.

"Well, come on," Po said. "Will is alone in the forest. We'd better find him." Again, the ghost sounded faintly regretful. And in fact Po would have liked nothing more than to leave Will languishing in the dark and cold on his own.

"I really don't know what I would do without you," Liesl said, with a rush of gratitude, as they set off into the forest. "I don't know what I *did* without you. Now that we've found each other, you'll never leave, will you?"

Po did not answer, but Liesl took his silence for agreement, and was happy.

TWENTY-SIX

WILL HEARD A TWIG SNAP BEHIND HIM. HE whirled around, brandishing a stick like a sword, and cried out, "Who's there?"

"It's all right, Will." Liesl stepped out from behind a tree, followed by Po and Bundle. "It's just us."

Will lowered the stick, feeling slightly foolish. "I thought you might be the alchemist or the Lady Premiere."

"The alchemist?" Liesl wrinkled her nose. "The one you used to work with?" While they were traveling from Cloverstown, Will had told her, in broad terms, about his work with the alchemist, although he had not confessed to being a lowly apprentice.

Will explained, "The alchemist and the Lady Premiere are after me, for losing a box of magic. The Lady Premiere was in disguise at Evergreen; she's the one who dragged you into the house. I'm afraid I started this whole thing." It was the first time Will had admitted to Liesl the real reason he had run away, and he hung his head.

Liesl rushed to reassure him. "It's not your fault. My stepmother's after me. She wants me dead." Liesl bit her lip, puzzling it out. "I wonder how they knew where to find us. I wonder how they knew we were together. . . ."

"The Lady Premiere knows everything, I expect," Will said glumly.

"She can't know *everything*," Liesl said. "She doesn't know I escaped, for example. Is the box safe?"

Will nodded. "I hid it." He stood on his tiptoes, reached into the large hollow of a massive oak tree, and extracted the box. "My plan was to . . ."

He trailed off, embarrassed. His plan was to hide the box and come to Liesl's rescue, and before she arrived, he had been working on building a ladder out of twigs and whatever else he could find, but he had not gotten very far. He shuffled a little closer to the clumsy beginnings of his construction, hoping she would not notice.

But it was too late.

"What on earth," Po demanded, "is *that*?" The ghost,

recovered from its earlier exertion, showed quite clearly against the heavy black darkness of the forest. Now it flitted around the pile of sticks Will had begun to assemble and tie together, painstakingly, with hanging vines.

"Nothing," Will said quickly, trying to block Liesl's view. But she sidestepped him.

"Is that"—she wrinkled her nose—"is that a ladder?"

Will decided there was no point in pretending otherwise. "Yes," he said miserably. "Po told me they had you up in one of the high rooms."

"And you were going to rescue me?" Liesl asked.

"Yes," Will mumbled. "Or try to, at least." His face was burning hot. He had never been so embarrassed in his life; he saw now how stupid the idea was. And obviously she didn't need rescuing—she had gotten out all on her own. The alchemist had, perhaps, been right all along. He *was* useless.

Suddenly Liesl threw her arms around him with such force that he stumbled backward. Will had never been hugged in all his life, and he did not know what to do. Liesl's hair tickled his cheek, and he could feel her little heart, beating hard through layers of cloth and clothing. He stood perfectly still, praying that she would let him go, feeling even more embarrassed than he had been just a moment earlier.

"Thank you," she said. "I think you're very brave."

"You do?"

"Yes. And clever."

"Oh." When Liesl released him at last, Will found that his head felt strange and fuzzy, as though he had just been spinning in a circle. He repeated, "Oh."

Po made a loud sniffing sound.

Liesl was feeling hopeful again. "Come," she said. "We can't be far from the Red House now. But it won't be long before they discover I'm missing and come looking for us."

"If they're not *already* looking for us," Will said.

"All the more reason to get moving," Po said, and as usual, it took the lead with Bundle.

The wind was a strange one that night: It blew strong, and smelled of difference and change. It sent shivers snaking up people's backs; it made old women tug their shawls closer, and babies cry, and maids rise from their beds to check that the shutters were definitely latched.

Will and Liesl felt it. Pausing to rest for a bit, they had to huddle together in the shelter of a maple, and still they felt deeply chilled, as though the wind wanted something from them and had reached inside to get it.

Augusta felt it creeping through the floorboards of Evergreen Manor, seeping in through the walls and past the windowsills, and it filled her with nameless terror, and made her rush upstairs to check on Liesl, who was, of course, no longer there. . . .

The alchemist and the Lady Premiere, racing through the woods with their lanterns held aloft, felt it. Mrs. Snout felt it, and it brought to her a sense of regret, though she could not have said why.

Sticky, on his way to the Red House, felt it, and found he was not even warmed by thoughts of what he would do with his newfound wealth. . . .

A policeman, a sneezing old woman, and a thickheaded guard carrying a cat in a sling all felt it, as they set off through the foothills in pursuit of Will and Liesl. They had just met on the road a one-eyed boy on a donkey, who had, in response to their question about two children, replied dutifully with the phrase Mrs. Snout had made him repeat. *"The children are on their way to the Red House. . . ."*

The policeman muttered a curse under his breath and pulled his scarf tighter.

The old woman sneezed, and stared bleakly at the cat in the sling.

The cat shivered.

The guard fingered the hat in his pocket.

The boy on the donkey thought of his missing eye, and roundedness, and a world undivided.

And all around them, tremendous magic continued to swirl and spiral and scatter, carried on by the wind.

TWENTY-SEVEN

LIESL AND WILL MADE THEIR WAY OUT OF THE
forest with Po and Bundle scouting. By the time the trees
thinned and the land became flat and empty again, morning had come. The sky was the color of new milk, one long
sheet of clouds stretched tight. Still the wind blew, hard and
strange, stirring up old feelings and memories.

"I know where we are," Liesl said. The edge of the forest,
the hard, flat fields in front of them, the dry creek bed they
came upon, the wind: All of it brought her tumbling head-
long into her past. She was falling, flailing, as images came
rushing back: the smell of new damp earth and wild grasses
to her waist; running toward the pond, which flashed like
a coin beyond the willow tree; the old well with its moss-
covered stones; laughter and shouting; the creaks of the old

house, the way it swelled in the rain like an old woman's joints; endless games of hide-and-seek; dark closets, and the smell of wool and mothballs.

There were other memories too, these more indistinct and also more puzzling, of the feeling of warmth tickling her neck, and a luminous and dazzling presence in the sky. The sun.

"The house is that way." Liesl pointed. She felt she must speak in a whisper, as though they were in church. "Just beyond the stone wall. The pond and the willow tree are a little past the house."

Perhaps Will felt, too, that the place they had come to was sacred. He bowed his head and began stepping carefully, as though worried he might cause the ground to shatter. Even Po was hesitant. In the watery daylight, the ghost was nothing more than a comma of gray air, flickering in and out uncertainly. Only Bundle turned merrily ahead, unaware.

Even though it was cold and the wind was raw, Liesl began to sweat as they crossed the field. The box slipped a little in her grip and she had to wipe her palms, one after another, against her jacket. They had traveled a long way to be exactly here, and yet Liesl had not given much thought to what would happen when she arrived and saw the house again after all these years. She had not given much thought, either, to what it would mean to put her father in the ground. Then she would truly be alone.

As if sensing her thoughts, Will whispered, "You all right?"

"Yes," Liesl whispered back, and adjusted the box in her arms. *No*, she thought. *Not alone. Not ever again.* She had Will and Po and Bundle now.

They reached the low stone wall. Bundle and Po passed through it absentmindedly; Will and Liesl scrambled after them. Beyond the wall, the land dipped. At the bottom of the gentle, sloping hill was the Red House, and beyond that was the pond, reflecting the flat, hard silver sky and the weeping willow tree. The tree's leaves were brown, and it looked more stooped and sad and saggy than ever.

"Oh," Liesl said, and "Oh" again. There was a hollow feeling in her chest. The house, the pond, the tree—it was all both overwhelmingly familiar and different from what she remembered—smaller and shabbier, somehow. It was like waking up to find that your reflection in the mirror had aged overnight, or had sprouted a new mole: You were forced to admit that things changed, whether you gave them permission to or not.

Liesl was overwhelmed by a sense of the otherness of everything. She belonged to the world, but the world did not belong to her; she was only the smallest, sprouting part of it, a tiny wart growing on the backside of an elephant. Somewhere there existed a glowing, magical, center part of the universe, but she was nowhere near it. The idea made her feel both comforted and sad at the same time.

"We used to have picnics there"—Liesl gestured to an empty place—"and in the winter we made snow angels there." She was alarmed to feel a lump building in her throat.

"Well." Will's voice was unnecessarily and deliberately cheery, and seemed out of place. "We might as well do what we came to—"

"Shhh," Po hushed him sharply. "I hear voices." In a second, Po and Bundle were gone.

Will and Liesl froze. They strained to listen, but could make out nothing above the howling wind and the pounding of their hearts.

Then Po and Bundle were back. Bundle was *mwark*ing excitedly. Po was very grave.

"It's them," Po said. "The one you called the Lady Premiere, and the thin man."

"The alchemist," Will gasped, turning white.

"Quickly," Liesl said, and started toward the house. They had come this far; they could not be stopped now. "There's a closet behind the stairs. We can hide there."

The windows of the Red House were covered with a thick layer of dust, and paint was flaking from its exterior, as though the house were slowly shedding its skin. But to Liesl's surprise the front door opened easily.

The alchemist and the Lady Premiere had just reached the stone wall when Liesl, Will, Bundle, and Po slipped into the house.

"Shut the door," Liesl whispered to Will, and he did. The windows were so grimy they admitted no light. Once the door was closed, Liesl could see absolutely nothing.

"Do you think they saw us?" Will whispered.

"I don't know," Liesl answered.

"Bundle and I will stand watch outside," Po said. "We will tell you if the lady and the thin man are headed for the house." Just like that, the ghosts were gone.

For a moment Will and Liesl stood inside the door, listening. They could hear the Lady Premiere and the alchemist speaking as they came down the hill, their footsteps crunching on the dew-coated grass.

"I see no signs of them," the Lady Premiere was saying.

"We may have beat them here," the alchemist responded.

"Come," Liesl whispered. "This way." She began to move very slowly toward the staircase at the back of the house, keeping both hands on the walls on either side of

her, feeling her way. Wallpaper crumbled beneath her fingertips: yellow wallpaper, covered with purple pansies, she
remembered. The house smelled like mildew and closeness,
and windows that had not been opened in ever so long. But
beneath it, Liesl thought she could detect another smell, one
she remembered from long ago: of freshly baked cookies,
and wild heather, and happiness.

Will stepped heavily behind Liesl, and a wooden board
creaked under his boot.

"Be *careful*," Liesl whispered.

"Sorry," Will whispered back.

They inched along through the pitch-black hall. Liesl
tried to remember the exact layout of the downstairs. That
must be the kitchen they were passing on the right—she
could feel the swinging doors, a different texture under her
fingertips—which meant that any second, on the left, they
would come to the dining room.

"*ACHOO!*"

"Bless you," both Will and Liesl said automatically, at
the same time.

"I didn't sneeze," Liesl said.

"I didn't either," Will said, fear creeping into his voice.
"Liesl, I think—"

The rest of his words were drowned out. Lanterns flashed

on around them, and suddenly the house was filled with shouting. A woman was crowing, "Found 'em at last! And didn't I know they'd be together!" Liesl and Will felt rough hands seize them—in their fear, they could not have said how many hands, nor how many bodies materialized from the darkness around them. Everything was confusion, an inhuman wailing almost like a cat's yowling, and a rapid stuttering of sneezes, one after another, and the walls lit up with dancing shadows.

Will saw an enormous face, white and terrible in the glow of a lantern. Its smile was as broad as a half-moon, and beneath it was another face—an animal's face—two bright yellow eyes and a small nose. Terrified, Will had the impression that the faces were fused together and he was staring at a two-headed demon.

"There you are," the upper face said. "I knew I'd catch up with you sooner or later. I have a little present for you."

Will saw two enormous hands coming toward him, holding a black piece of fabric. He thought, *I am going to be suffocated.*

He thought, *I am going to die now.*

And then, just as Mo slipped a heavy woolen hat on Will's head, he fainted.

TWENTY-EIGHT

FOR A FEW SECONDS AFTER AWAKENING, WILL did not know where he was. The small and faded room, the pain in his lower back, and the familiar mutterings of the alchemist made him think for a moment he was back at the alchemist's apartments, and the past few days—the misplaced magic, the flight, the train, and Liesl—had been a dream.

"Did you enjoy your nap?" Po asked sarcastically.

Will jumped, and immediately felt a sharp pain in his shoulders and wrists. The ghost flickered just to his left, then materialized on the other side of Liesl. Liesl and Will were sitting side by side in two rickety chairs. They had each been handcuffed with their arms behind them, and their ankles had been bound to the chairs with heavy rope.

Will felt his cheeks burn. He could not believe he had fainted in front of Liesl. "What—what happened?"

"We were ambushed," Liesl said dully. "And they've taken the box."

Will shook his head, trying to clear it. The oil fumes in the room—from several lanterns, placed at intervals on the wooden floor—made thinking difficult. Will guessed they were in the dining room. There was a long wooden table in the center of the room, surrounded by several chairs whose silk cushions were long faded to a dingy white, and torn apart by insects.

Standing in one corner were the old woman from the train, the policeman, and the guard from the Lady Premiere's town house. The guard was still carrying a cat in a sling around his chest. This, Will realized with a sense of shame, was the two-headed monster who had confronted him in the hall, the one who had so terrified Will in the dark.

The old woman seemed to be berating him. She jabbed her cane onto the wooden floor for emphasis.

"Of course it's necessary that they be kept under lock and key!" she was saying. "It's the definition of necessary! Those two—*ACHOO!*—are criminals, and we are doing our public duty by—*ACHOO!*—bringing them to justice!"

"Criminals, eh?" Mo was rubbing his forehead and looking confused. "They just look like two kids to me."

"A criminal disguise! Didn't you hear what the— ACHOO!—Lady Premiere said? In possession of stolen property! ACHOO! And fugitives to boot! ACHOO!"

"I don't know," Mo said doubtfully.

The door of the room banged open, admitting a gust of old, cold air. The Lady Premiere swept regally in from the hallway, followed by the alchemist.

"We will perform the ceremony here," she said, gesturing to the old dining room table. "I will see it work with my own eyes. There will be no mistakes this time."

"No, no," the alchemist hastened to assure her. "Absolutely none."

"We will wait for Augusta," the Lady Premiere said sharply, "since she has been so instrumental to us."

Next to Will, Liesl began to tremble. "Augusta's here," she whispered. "She means to kill me, I'm sure of it."

"I won't let her," Will said, with a confidence he did not feel. "Don't worry, Liesl. We'll figure out a way to escape."

"How?" Po flickered. "Do you intend to faint them into submission?"

"What we need is time." Liesl strained against the

handcuffs, then quickly gave up as the metal cut into her wrists. But perhaps if she could somehow get her legs free . . . "We need time to plan. Time to think."

"We need a distraction," Will said, remembering how he and the other orphans had sometimes set firecrackers off just outside the warden's window, whenever the warden was supposed to be paddling one of the boys for misbehavior, so the warden would be prevented from delivering the full forty swings.

"A distraction!" Liesl seized on the idea. "Po, do you think you might . . . ?"

But Po had disappeared, taking Bundle with it.

"Great." Will rolled his eyes. "Very brave."

"I'm sure Po will be back," Liesl said, but she sounded uneasy.

Footsteps rang sharply down the hall. Then Augusta swept into the room. She cast a withering glance around her, at the faded wallpaper that hung in patches and tatters, and the uneven wooden floor, and the old dining room table, and the insect-eaten cushions on the high-backed chairs, and wrinkled her nose in distaste.

"I had hoped never to return to this place," Augusta said. "It is just as hideous as I remembered."

"Hello, Augusta," the Lady Premiere said. "You're just in time. The alchemist is about to perform the magic."

"Magic!" the old lady from the train repeated. "Bah!" Then she sneezed.

"Magic!" Mo shook his head wonderingly. "Who'dve thought."

"Magic!" In spite of herself, Liesl was curious.

Augusta swiveled her head in Liesl's direction. "There you are, my pet. Safe and sound." She came across the room, her long skirts rustling against the wooden floor with a hissing sound that reminded Liesl of a snake. She placed a hand heavily on Liesl's shoulder and said in a low voice, "For the time being, at least. It will be a long journey back to Dirge, and these roads are very dangerous. I fear you will not make it."

Liesl jerked away from her stepmother's grasp and nearly toppled off her chair. Augusta laughed meanly.

"We are ready," the alchemist announced. "Where is the magic?"

"The only magic I'd like to see—*ACHOO!*—is the delivery of these two troublemakers to jail."

"Quiet!" the Lady Premiere thundered. She directed her fierce stare at the old woman and her two traveling companions. "I will permit you to stay because of your role in bringing these two thieves to justice. Especially you, sir. It is a credit to your loyalty." She nodded at Mo, who blushed bright red all the way up to his hair and cast a desperate glance at Will. Will refused to look at him, feeling he had been terribly betrayed.

"But," the Lady Premiere continued emphatically, "I must insist on absolute and total silence. If I hear so much as a peep from any of you, I can assure you, you will regret it."

The old lady sneezed surreptitiously into the sleeve of her coat. Mo went rapidly from red to white. Even the policeman seemed to shrink guiltily backward, like a young boy with his hand caught in the cookie jar.

The Lady Premiere smiled tightly. "Much better." She lowered herself into a chair at the head of the table.

"The potion, if you please," said the alchemist. His hands were trembling slightly. It was time! Time, at last, to prove what he was capable of.

With great ceremony, the Lady Premiere withdrew the wooden box she had confiscated from Liesl and placed it carefully on the table in front of the alchemist.

Liesl gave a small cry of surprise. "That isn't magic,"

she said, startled into speaking out. "You've got everything mixed up. That's my father. We carried him here, to bury him next to the willow tree."

"Your father?" The Lady Premiere narrowed her eyes. She believed Liesl to be the servant girl Vera, as Augusta had claimed.

"Don't listen to her," Augusta jumped in. "The girl is full of lies. She conspired with the boy to steal the potion; she is only pretending to be confused, thinking you will spare her."

"Then she does not know me," the Lady Premiere said coldly. "There is no point in playing innocent with me, you poisonous wretch. You know as well as I do that the boxes were switched. What you've had with you all this time is nothing less than the greatest magic in the world."

"In the universe!" the alchemist piped up.

Will was filled with a sense of wonder as the meaning of everything that had happened became clear. He remembered the two wooden boxes sitting side by side on Mr. Gray's table, and how sleepy he was when he confused them. All at once, Will realized his error: He had taken Liesl's father's ashes to the Lady Premiere, and he and Liesl had been in possession of the real magic all along.

"It was an accident," Will squeaked.

"It was treasonous!" the alchemist hissed.

"I don't understand," Liesl murmured. She was truly and hopelessly confused. "Where are my father's ashes?"

"I have taken care of them." Augusta bent down to speak quietly in Liesl's ear. "Do not trouble your pretty little head about that."

Liesl turned pale. "What did you do?" she whispered fiercely.

Augusta's smile was like the wide grin of a piranha: humorless, and all teeth. "I have shored him up tightly behind a downstairs wall, where he can keep company with the slick and the slime and the deep and the damp and the creepy, crawly things, and where he will be always and forever in the dark."

"You're a monster." Liesl could barely get the words out. The room underneath her chair seemed to be swinging wildly from side to side. She worried for a moment that she might be dying—and then for another terrible moment, felt she wouldn't care if she were.

"Enough dawdling!" the Lady Premiere barked. She gestured to a chair on her left. "Augusta, if you please."

Augusta inclined her head graciously and swept to the

Lady Premiere's side. "My pleasure," she cooed, settling her massive girth into the narrow chair, which creaked and moaned under her weight.

"And now . . ." The Lady Premiere folded her hands in her lap. But she was anything but calm; she eyed the wooden box with the greed of a cat eyeing an injured mouse. "The magic, if you please."

The room was utterly silent.

The old lady stopped sneezing.

Will and Liesl held their breath.

And the alchemist opened the box.

TWENTY-NINE

A FUNNY THING HAPPENED WHEN THE ALCHEMIST saw, instead of the missing magic that had been the start of all his trouble—magic made from summer afternoons, from laughter and snowflakes, magic distilled from the sun!— a mound of worthless powder that looked suspiciously like potato flour: He felt in that moment as though his insides, too, had been turned to flour, all dry and crumbly. For a second he worried he would disintegrate into a pile on the floor. Then, feeling the weight of the Lady Premiere's eyes on him, he almost *wished* he would.

"Well?" the Lady Premiere demanded eagerly. "How does it look?"

"Oh—all in order. Yes, absolutely. Very magic," the alchemist stammered, angling his body slightly so that the contents of the box were concealed from the Lady's view. His mind was cycling furiously. He knew without doubt that if he were to admit to the Lady Premiere that the magic had once again been lost, it would be very, very bad for him. She had already threatened several times to consign him to the darkest, dampest corners of her dungeons, and provide him free lodgings among her rats, should he fail to recover the magic that had been promised her.

"Are you going to get on with it or what?" the Lady Premiere prodded him.

"Patience, dear Lady," the alchemist said, licking sweat from his upper lip. "Magic is a very finicky thing. It cannot be rushed."

The Lady Premiere settled back in her chair, grumbling. The alchemist mopped his forehead with his sleeve.

Time. What he needed was time.

Across the room, Liesl was thinking exactly the same thing. Moving her ankles continuously back and forth, she felt a slight loosening of the ropes. She had to move ever so slowly: Periodically, Augusta swiveled to fix her with a terrible stare, and she could feel the old woman's eyes on her as well. If only Po would come back! Perhaps it could make itself visible, as it had just before they escaped from the attic. How long ago that seemed.

The alchemist began muttering to himself. It sounded to Liesl's ears as though he were reciting a spell or incantation. At least, she thought, the attention was now firmly on him. If she could somehow manage to swing her body around toward Will, perhaps he could help her jimmy the handcuffs. . . .

A small blue flame appeared in the air, hovering just above the alchemist's outstretched palm. He continued murmuring under his breath, and it swelled to a melon-sized ball of flame.

The Lady Premiere half rose from her seat; a small gasp went around the room. Even Liesl stopped fidgeting and stared.

It was real. The alchemist was doing magic.

"Now," the Lady Premiere said, and her eyes reflected twin orange balls of fire. "Call up the dead."

This was what the alchemist had feared. He had hoped to keep the Lady Premiere distracted with a simple fire charm. He always carried some flame-wood and a small quantity of sparking potion with him when he traveled, and he had prayed that this little display would buy him some time to think.

Now, he knew, he could no longer pretend. He would have to tell the truth.

The ball of fire floating in the air flared, as the alchemist opened his mouth. "The magic . . . ," he started to say. *The magic is lost.*

But he did not finish his sentence.

All of a sudden, the room seemed to *blink*. The empty air shivered, and flexed, and then opened like a mouth, revealing a long, dark throat.

Liesl recognized the dark space at once: It was a tunnel to the Other Side.

The Lady Premiere stood up all the way, so quickly she overturned her chair, which fell to the ground with a clatter.

The alchemist gaped.

The old woman sneezed.

Unseen, Po strained to hold open the entrance between sides.

And then the ghosts came howling through the tunnel, with the whirling, swirling energy of a thousand winds, and everything was chaos.

THIRTY

PO HAD SEEN THE NEED FOR A DISTRACTION EVEN before Will had suggested it. And so at the first opportunity, the ghost had slipped back to the Other Side.

Plan, Bundle, the ghost had thought to its companion. *What we need is a plan.*

Mwark, Bundle thought back, even more emphatically than usual.

They were in a place of towering skyscrapers built out of sheer black rock. Souls drifted around them, a dark mist. Po saw a line of the newly dead approaching from a distance: dozens of them, looking bewildered, speaking out loud in grating, almost human voices.

"Where are we?"

"I don't understand. I just went out to the store to get some butter."

"Aunt Carol always *said* that cities were dangerous. . . ."

Poor, lost new souls. As Po watched them get closer, it was filled with a sensation that felt like dispersing but was emptier and bigger, somehow: as though its Essence was evaporating into nothing.

Po knew what Liesl would call it. She would call it sadness. The voices, the new souls, came closer.

"This isn't like any place I've ever seen. Maybe it's New York? I hear they have big buildings in New York."

All those new ghosts: All they wanted was to go back to the Living Side, and back, too, in time—back to health and happiness, or even pain and sickness and poverty, so long as they were *alive*.

Then, suddenly, Po had an idea.

It had opened a door for Liesl, so that she could cross to the Other Side.

It would open one now, so that the ghosts could cross back.

Po focused its thoughts into sound.

"Hello!" it called out, against the black expanse of space. "Hello! You there!"

The new ghosts stopped marching. They squinted at Po, confused, and their voices became low murmurs.

"Now who is that, do you think?"

"I can't seem to make him out. Or is it a her?"

"Everything looks a bit fuzzy. Does it look fuzzy to you? My doctor *did* say my eyes were going. . . ."

The Living Side was folded up against the place where Po was standing, separated by only a very thin membrane of existence, and from it Po could feel Liesl's pulsing desperation, her need for escape. From it, too, he could hear a distant chanting, and see a glowing warm ball of light—no, of fire—which grew larger and larger, and filled Po's Essence with a sense of heat and urgency.

Po did not know how many laws of the universe it was about to break, but the ghost put the thought out of its mind.

"Here," Po said. "The path you are looking for is this way."

The new souls murmured and rustled, repeating the word *path* to themselves in confusion. Po thought for a moment it would not be able to go through with the dishonesty, with the tearing—but then Liesl's need came pulsing through the tissue-thin layers between worlds again, and the ball of fire burned like a beacon.

For the second time in the long, long course of its death, Po lied.

"This way," the ghost said, "will take you home."

And on the final word, he pulled. He strained and dug and stretched, and the space between the Other Side and the Living Side became a huge, yawning hole.

And the ghosts, responding to the promise of that simple word *home*—which carried inside of it as much magic, certainly, as the Lady Premiere could ever wish for—began streaming and tumbling out.

Because the ghosts were very new ghosts, they had not started to blend yet, and so were quite visible. And yet they were very clearly ghosts: Some had holes in their faces, or were missing arms or legs, where their physical selves had begun to dissipate and merge with the rest of the universe. As Will watched in wonder and horror, an old man came apart in front of his very eyes, like a drawing of a person being smudged into an indistinct blob of color.

It was not clear who was more confused, the ghosts or the living people. Already, they were not used to the Living Side, and its confusion of light and color and heavy smells and textures and *feelings*, and they found themselves even more disoriented than they had been a moment before. They were like wild animals pushed into a pen; they whirled and bumped one another and shrieked.

The old woman began screaming, which brought on another sneezing fit. The policeman tried to climb out a window, which was unfortunately stuck. Augusta toppled out of her chair and lay on her back, pedaling the air with her legs and beating at the ghosts with her hands and crying, "Mercy! Have mercy on us!"

Only the Lady Premiere stood stock-still in the middle of the room, her hands pressed to her sides, her face glowing with emotion. "It works," she whispered. "The magic works."

The alchemist was so startled he lost control of the fire. Whipped from his hands by the tremendous tumult of moving ghosts, it shot across the room and exploded. Suddenly one whole wall was covered in flames. Fire tore up the old wallpaper toward the ceiling; flames raced down toward the wooden floor, hungry, burning higher and higher, fed by the rush of air and motion. Ghosts became flame and then people again. Then they were merely shapes.

The heat made Liesl's eyes water, and her mouth was filled with the taste of ash.

"We have to get out of here!" she screamed to Will, bouncing her chair closer to his. "We'll be cooked like dumplings!"

Will rattled his handcuffs in frustration and kicked as hard as he could, trying to detach his ankles from the chair legs to which they had been bound. The chair teetered and fell over, and Will lay coughing and choking on the floor, as flames raced along the wooden boards toward his face. Already, he could hardly see. The room was full of dark, thick, roiling smoke, and smoky shapes moving within it.

"Will!" Liesl screamed. Her voice sounded very distant.

Then there was another voice, closer, and the feeling of something pulling at his legs.

"Hang on a second," the voice was saying. "Just a few little snips and you'll be all right." It was the Lady Premiere's guard; Will looked down and saw him sawing with a pocketknife at the ropes binding Will's ankles. Then, just like that, the ropes snapped and Will was free. Or at least, he could walk. The handcuffs were still cutting into his wrists.

The guard helped Will to his feet, then knelt and freed Liesl's ankles with a few slashes of his knife. Her head was slumped forward on her chest. The whole room was consumed with flame.

Will could no longer see the alchemist or the Lady Premiere or Augusta or the policeman—all he saw was burning, burning, burning. The fire was out of control.

It was in the cellar, and racing into the second floor, and licking into the attic.

"No time to stand around gaping," Mo said, and Will felt himself roughly dragged forward by the collar. "Too hot for my tastes."

Mo swung Liesl out of her chair with his free hand, and pressed her to his chest. Then, keeping Will, Liesl, and Lefty protected, he crashed back-first through the dining room windows and, amid an explosion of shattering glass, charged into the cool air outside.

THIRTY-ONE

ONCE LIESL WAS OUTSIDE AND AWAY FROM THE smoke, she revived.

"Po," she said, with her first intake of breath.

"It's all right," the ghost said. "I'm right here." Po was still very weak and its voice sounded faint, but Liesl was comforted.

"Where's Bundle?" Liesl asked.

A shaggy shape flickered momentarily in the air. Bundle was tired too. It had herded the ghosts back through the opening and returned them to the Other Side, and Po had closed up the door.

"I'm all right too," Will said, somewhat annoyed that the ghosts had been Liesl's first concern.

"Everybody's in tip-top shape," Mo said cheerfully. He

ignored the fact that their clothes were black with smoke, their faces streaked with ash, and their wrists cuffed behind their backs. "Even Lefty here is happy as a clam. Though she might be happier *with* a clam." Mo laughed at his own joke as the cat in the sling looked up at him—disapprovingly, Will thought. Then Mo leaned down to Will and whispered conspiratorially, "I only wanted to give you the hat, so's you wouldn't be cold."

"The house!" Liesl cried out. They were sitting at the edge of the pond, by the old willow tree, where Mo had felt they would be safe, and Liesl had looked behind her for the first time. "The whole house is burning!"

The fire, driven now by that strange and unfamiliar wind, which had blown the real magic all across the countryside, had reached the very top of the peaked roof.

"I'm afraid so," Mo said. "From the crown to the cellar. There won't be nothing to it but ash."

"The cellar . . ." Something had just occurred to Liesl, and she turned to Will, eyes shining. "Augusta buried my father's ashes behind a wall. Remember? She said so. But now even the walls are burning."

Will nodded solemnly. "It looks like he'll make it to the willow tree after all, Liesl."

Liesl squeezed her fists tightly. "Let it burn," she whispered. "Let the whole thing burn down to the last piece of wood."

At exactly that moment—as the Lady Premiere and the alchemist were staggering toward them, leaning on each other, and Augusta was running toward the pond with her shoelaces on fire, screaming, and the old woman was riding the policeman's back as though he were a pony, and beating him with her cane to make him go faster—the house gave an enormous shudder, and with a tremendous rolling crack collapsed in on itself.

The walls came down. Wood turned to smoke and ash. The contents of the little wooden box were released, and drifted upward on tendrils of wind and air—upward and outward, over the sloping hill, and down toward the slate-gray water of the pond—and to the velvet-soft ground beneath the willow tree, where they should have been all along.

Somehow, Liesl *knew*. She felt that the ashes had been returned, and as the last recognizable part of her old home was consumed in flame, she began to cry. But she was not sad; she was filled with joy and relief.

After all that, she had done what she had set out to do. She had brought her father home so he could rest.

Po and Will looked at each other helplessly. The single tear Liesl had shed in the hills had been bad enough, they both thought. This display of emotion was quite beyond the both of them.

It was Mo who squatted down beside Liesl and began to comfort her. "There, there." He patted her shoulder heavily. "It's going to be okay."

Liesl could not explain that she was crying mostly out of happiness, so instead she just nodded.

Augusta charged into the shallows of the pond, skirts hitched up to her knees, where her shoelaces were at last extinguished. She let out a loud howl of satisfaction and sloshed back up to the grass, where she collapsed ungracefully onto her rump. The sight of the ghosts had so unnerved her that she had temporarily forgotten about her stepdaughter. She whipped out a handkerchief and began mopping her face, repeatedly muttering, "Mercy. Mercy."

The old woman and the policeman had reached the pond as well, and the old woman had dismounted. Now that the fire was smoldering far behind them, and the house no more than a black, smoking pile of soot, the old woman felt able to express her outrage.

"Well, I never!" She gesticulated wildly in the air with

her cane. "In all my life! It ought to be illegal! I'll take it up with the judge!" Without saying so directly, she made it clear that she was referring to magic; and fire; and ghosts; and the whole business.

The Lady Premiere's head was filled with visions of power. She imagined an army of ghosts; with it she could take over the whole world!

"Again," she croaked to the alchemist. "I want to see them again. I want you to call up the ghosts!"

"H-here?" the alchemist stammered. Nobody had been more staggered by the ghosts' appearance than he. Was it possible—conceivable—that he had, in fact, performed the Great Magic? It must be so! And yet he had done nothing out of the ordinary but wish for the magic to occur and the ghosts to appear.

An idea, a pleasurable thought, began winking in the alchemist's brain. Perhaps he was even more powerful than he had ever known.

"Here and now." The Lady Premiere was very pale, but her eyes glowed like stars. She looked like someone in the grip of a very high fever. "I must know. I must be sure."

"You can't!" the old woman spluttered. "You won't! It's an outrage!"

Nobody bothered to answer her. An uneasy hush fell over the assembled group. Liesl and Will knew that the ghosts had come through the door Po had opened— Po had told them so—but still, they couldn't help but feel as though something great was about to occur. Unconsciously, they leaned forward, keeping their eyes locked on the alchemist.

And indeed, there did seem to be some kind of magical, shifting quality to the air. Even the alchemist felt it: a power growing and swelling around him.

Of course, what he could not know—what none of them knew—was that the magic *was* there. It was everywhere, unseen, shimmering, waiting to be called up. It was floating on the wind and skimming over the hard, dry earth; it was hanging like a curtain just beyond the visible world.

The alchemist was not sure how he had called up the ghosts in the first place, so he did not know exactly what to do to raise them again. He took a deep breath and spoke out the words to the magic: *"The dead will rise from glade to glen and ancient will be young again."*

His voice rolled and echoed in the silence. For a moment, no one spoke.

Then the Lady Premiere growled, "Nothing's happening."

The alchemist giggled nervously. "I don't know what could have possibly—"

Liesl hushed him. "Look!" she cried out. "Something *is* happening."

She was right. Something *was* happening. That unseen curtain of magic draped everywhere and over everything all at once—that fine, invisible layer—became visible for one white-hot second. The air appeared suddenly to take on the quality of a rainbow, layered with color after color. Will gasped; Liesl cried out; the old woman made the sign of the cross.

Then the earth began to shake.

"What's happening?" shrieked Augusta.

The alchemist and the Lady Premiere were thrown off their feet. The alchemist landed on top of the Lady and became entangled in her fur.

"Get off me!" she screamed, kicking at him.

"Is it an earthquake?" Liesl asked.

"It's the magic," Po said, and its voice was full of wonder.

Then a column of gold, a finger of light, appeared. It stretched from the sky to the very center of the pond like a long, flaming braid binding them together—flashing, blindingly bright. At this even the Lady Premiere fell silent.

All at once the hard, cold earth seemed to explode. The brown surface of the world dissolved and in its place was an impossible, an inconceivable, an unbelievable profusion of color: green grass and purple and red flowers; sprays of lily; white baby's breath that covered the hills; nodding fields of bright yellow daffodils; rich purple moss. The trees burst forth with new leaves. The weeping willow tree was a mass of tiny pale green leaves, thousands of them, which whispered and sighed together as the wind moved through its branches. There were fat heads of lettuce in the fields, and cucumbers lying like jewels among them, and enormous red tomatoes surrounded by thick, knotted vines.

And for the first time in more than 1,728 days, the clouds broke apart and there was dazzling blue sky, and light beyond what anyone could remember.

The sun had come out at last.

Liesl squinted and laughed. Will ducked his head, blinking back tears, embarrassed; he told himself it was just a reaction to the sudden brightness.

Mo took off his hat and pressed it to his chest. Lefty jumped from her sling and began batting at a butterfly. The old woman fell to her knees and remembered what it was like to be young, and wept.

"Isn't it amazing?" Liesl could not stop laughing. "It's like a dream. It's better than a dream!"

The alchemist sat dazed and dumbfounded, as the true meaning of the magic was revealed: *The dead will rise from glade to glen and ancient will be young again.* The dead had, after all, risen. From dead and dry things there was growth, and new life everywhere. And the endlessly long winter had at last turned to spring.

From life to death and back again to life. It was indeed the greatest magic in the world.

The alchemist decided, at that moment, to retire.

At that moment, too, Augusta began screaming.

"No! Please, no! Stay away from me!" She had raised herself on her knees and was staring out over the pond, holding both hands protectively in front of her.

Liesl's mouth turned to chalk. Her heart skipped in her chest.

The figure of a man was walking across the surface of the water.

And even though he was translucent, and the sunlight reflecting up from the pond rendered him the glassy-colored hue of a soap bubble, Liesl knew him right away.

"Father," she croaked out.

He looked at her. "Hello, Lee-Lee," he said in his old, kind voice. Liesl's heart shook itself out and rose like a butterfly.

"Evil!" Augusta was scrabbling frantically backward, like an overgrown crab. "Evil! Unnatural! Stay away from me!"

The ghost of Henry Morbower whirled on her. Its voice turned low and furious. "How dare you use that word? The only evil here is your own."

Augusta turned sheet-white. "No!" she shrieked as the ghost continued to advance toward her. "Please! Have mercy!"

"Why should I? You showed no mercy to me."

"An accident." Augusta began to tremble. "It was an accident."

"Liar!"

"I didn't mean to! I only wanted you to be sick—just a little sick, so you'd be out of the way!" Augusta's voice rose hysterically.

"Lies again!" the ghost of Henry Morbower thundered. "You are a liar and a murderer!"

Augusta looked around her frantically, searching for a means of escape. Her eyes were huge and wild. She went from resembling a crab to a cornered rat.

"You!" She pointed at the alchemist. "It's all your fault! You gave me the poison!"

"I—I—I—" the alchemist spluttered nervously. "I did no such thing."

"You did! 'Pernicious Poison: Dead as a Doorknob, or Your Money Back!' Written right on the label!"

"Dead as a doorknob?" repeated the old woman sharply. She had quite recovered from her earlier display of emotion. She struck the policeman with her cane. "Did you hear that? A common murderer! She must be arrested at once—for the Common Good!"

"Well, I never," Mo said, scratching his head.

"My dear lady." The alchemist seemed about to deny it. He stood, brushing off his cloak indignantly, and drew himself up to his full height.

Then he turned, holding his hat tightly to his head with one hand, and began dashing up the hill.

The old woman gave the policeman a sharp *thwack* on the shins. "Go on! Get after him! It's criminal, I tell you. Making poison and hanging around with ghosts. He should be ashamed." She sniffed loudly.

The policeman began dutifully chasing after the alchemist.

The ghost of Henry Morbower turned back to his daughter. He smiled. "It's beautiful here, isn't it, Lee-Lee?

Do you remember how we used to have picnics by the pond? And you would always try and climb the tree, but you were too small for even its lowest branches."

She nodded. There was an enormous lump in her throat. She couldn't talk her way around it. "Father . . . ," she said.

"I know, Lee-Lee." Rays of light shone through the translucence. "It makes me ineffably happy as well."

"Yes." Liesl nodded. "Yes, ineffably."

The ghost of Henry Morbower wavered, and became for a second no more than a shadow-impression; then it reappeared. Its head was tilted. It seemed to be listening. "I have to go now, Lee-Lee. Be good."

"I'll miss you," Liesl croaked out.

"I'll be here," the ghost of Henry Morbower said, and then all at once was nothing more than air, and a few drifting golden petals that landed at Liesl's feet.

For a moment no one said anything. In the silence, Liesl sniffed and ducked her head so no one would see the tears snaking their way over her cheeks and down toward the tip of her nose. Everyone did see, but pretended not to notice.

Then Will cried out sharply, "It's Augusta! She's getting away!"

While everyone's attention was riveted by the ghost,

Augusta had been attempting to crawl away from the pond. Now, hearing Will's shout, she sprang to her feet and began sprinting. She was surprisingly quick, despite her bulk and the long skirts she was wearing.

The policeman, who was steering the alchemist by the elbows down the hill, groaned. "Not another one," he said. "Not again."

"I'll get her!" Mo said, quite pleased to have something useful to do. He had always fantasized that someday he would be part of a high-speed chase to catch a murderer, even though he was only a lowly guard. Now his dreams were coming true. He bounded off.

Liesl swiped her eyes with her forearm. Something had just occurred to her. "Where's Po?" she asked. "Where's Bundle?"

The air was empty all around them. Will shook his head, shrugging.

"Over here, Liesl!"

Liesl turned her head and gasped.

There, standing a little ways off on a large sun-drenched portion of grass, were Po and Bundle. Or at least, they were Po- and Bundle-*shaped*; and yet instead of their usual shad-owy, indistinct forms, they appeared to be growing bodies again, expanding into solid shapes. They were golden—they'd been dipped in gold—no—they were made *of* gold. And then the golden Po-shape turned into tan brown arms and shoulders, and a ring of curly yellow hair, and a laughing smile, and the golden Bundle-shape turned into a small, bounding, yellow mass of fur. A dog.

Po was looking at Liesl. Liesl suddenly felt shy.

Po said, "Boy." Then he stretched out his fingers, wiggling them. "Peter. My name is Peter."

Bundle went, *"Bark, bark."*

"Thank you, Liesl," the boy Peter said, laughing.

"For what?" Liesl started to ask, but she was asking to emptiness. The boy and the dog had disappeared, just like that.

"Where did they go?" Liesl demanded, to no one in particular. "What happened?"

"I think—," Will said. "I think they must have gone on."

"To Beyond," Liesl said, and knew that it was true. For a moment she felt as if the breath had been knocked out of her. There was an aching in her throat, and the world around her seemed very empty.

"It's the way of things, you know," Will whispered to her, as though reading her mind. "It's how it ought to be."

"I know," Liesl whispered back. And she did, really, deep down. "It's just—"

"What?"

"I don't know where to go. I don't know what comes now."

"Don't worry," Will said. "We'll figure something out."

Liesl managed to smile at him. She liked that word: *we*. It sounded warm and open, like a hug.

"Got 'er," Mo called out. He had caught up with Augusta and was holding her tightly, as she wriggled and kicked and tried to squirm her way out of his grasp: Now she was a fish on a hook.

The old woman adjusted her hat more firmly on her head and brushed off her velvet coat. "Well," she sniffed. "I think we've had quite enough for the day—of ghosts and criminals and fires and all that nonsense. Go on and cuff them and take them in." She gestured to the alchemist and Augusta.

"I can't," the policeman said meekly. In his short time with the old woman, he had grown quite terrified of displeasing her.

She fixed him with a fierce glare. "Why ever not?"

He ducked his head guiltily. "Only have two pairs of cuffs."

Liesl and Will exchanged a hopeful look and tried to look as innocent as possible.

The old woman stared at them witheringly for a moment. "I see. Very unfortunate. Well, in that case, I suppose we ought to let the children go. We can't have poison makers and murderers running around the countryside, can we? It goes entirely against common sense and decency."

The policeman, still dragging the pathetic alchemist by an elbow, extracted a key from his vest and squatted down to unlock Will and Liesl's handcuffs. The moment they were released they stood up, rubbing their sore wrists. Liesl threw her arms around Will and he patted her once, awkwardly, on the back, and turned as red as the tomatoes in the field.

The policeman placed handcuffs on the alchemist and Augusta and escorted both prisoners up the hill. For a long time, Liesl could still hear Augusta protesting her innocence and the alchemist muttering about conspiracies and useless apprentices—until the wind and the flapping of butterflies and the birdsong took over, and finally she couldn't hear their voices at all.

"Well." The Lady Premiere frowned. "I, for one, am not going to stand around here all day. I am the Lady Premiere, and the most powerful woman in the city, and I have business to take care of."

"Lady Premiere?" came a voice from farther up the hill. "Is that what you're calling yourself nowadays? Pretty fancy title for a fisherman's daughter."

A black-haired man had just climbed the stone wall and was striding down the hill toward the pond. Will and Liesl both recognized him immediately as the man they had seen eating soup at Mrs. Snout's inn. He was staring fixedly at the Lady Premiere, and his smile was huge and villainous.

The Lady Premiere went as white as paper and began to tremble. All at once, she smelled cabbages everywhere. It was all-consuming. She was choking on it. The narrow and cramped rooms of her childhood home rose up around her, a specter of poverty and smallness.

"No!" she gasped. "It—it can't be. I thought you must be dead."

"You wished I was, you mean." Sticky narrowed his eyes.

"What are you doing here?" The Lady Premiere sounded as though a bullfrog had been lodged in her throat. "How did you find me? What do you want?"

Sticky spread his arms, still grinning. "Thought it might be time for a little family reunion with my older sister."

"Sister!" Mo said, scratching his head.

"Sister!" the old woman sniffed, looking the raggedy black-haired man up and down with disdain.

"Sister!" Will and Liesl cried simultaneously.

Sticky eyed the Lady Premiere's fur coat, and the diamonds winking in her ears, and the large rings on her fingers. He had already forgotten about the little girl and the wooden box. What a lucky day! He had come for the girl's jewelry and had instead stumbled on a much, much larger fortune. "I see you've done pretty well for yourself, Gretchen."

"Don't call me that!" the Lady Premiere screeched.

Will coughed. He had never considered that the Lady Premiere had even had a first name. And Gretchen was so . . . plain.

"Now don't tell me you've forgotten your name," Sticky said, and then began to singsong, "Gross and rotten, wretched Gretchen!"

"Stop it!" the Lady Premiere shrieked.

"Gretchen the grodiest wretch in the Glen!"

"I—said—stop!"

"Excuse me, sir," Mo put in. He liked the Lady Premiere less now than ever, but since he was still technically in her employ, he felt it appropriate to speak up on her behalf. "I think you might have your wires crossed somewhere. The Lady Premiere is a Very Important Person. She is a royal, too. A princess from Sweden. No, no. From Norway. No, that's not right. From Italy, if I recall correctly. . . ." Mo trailed off, feeling even more muddled than usual.

Sticky snorted. "A princess? So that's the story she's cooked up for herself, is it? Princess of flounder, maybe. A fisherman's daughter, no more and no less. Used to help pick the bones out of the sardines."

"Well!" The old woman shook her head. "Well, I never. A fisherman's daughter! Very out of the ordinary. *Quite* unheard of."

The Lady Premiere was so enraged she could hardly speak. "Shut up!" she screamed. "Shut up or I'll——"

"Or you'll what?" Sticky interjected, stepping so close to his sister they were practically nose-to-nose. "I'm not afraid of you anymore. If you want to keep your fishy little past a secret, you're going to have to pay."

The Lady Premiere suddenly seized Sticky by his left ear. He let out a yowl of pain.

"Listen, you squirming, squiggling little vermin," she hissed. "If you think I'll let you bully or blackmail me——"

"Let go of me!" Sticky twisted out of his sister's grasp. She darted forward and seized his right elbow. Sticky shouted, "Stop it! Stop pinching me!"

"What? What's that? You want me to *keep* pinching you?"

"No! Stop! No!" Sticky was backing up the hill, swatting at his sister's hands, as she continued to try and pinch and pull and tug at his earlobes, cheeks, and elbows.

"It's opposite day! No means yes!"

"Then yes! Yes—please keep pinching me!"

"Oh? You want more? *More* pinching?"

The two siblings were drawing farther and farther up the hill, hopping and twisting and slapping each other. From a distance they looked like two large, overgrown crickets performing a bizarre dance. When they reached the top of the hill, Sticky reached out and tugged sharply on the Lady Premiere's bun. She screeched, and made a lunge for him as he scrabbled over the stone wall.

Then they disappeared from view. It can be assumed that they spent the rest of their lives bullying and badgering, and teasing and tormenting, and irritating and insulting each other, until the end of their days; and furthermore, that they made each other quite as miserable as they both deserved to be.

For a moment there was silence, as Mo, Will, Liesl, and the old woman considered all they had seen. Then the old woman sniffed loudly.

"Harrumph. That's that, I suppose." She nodded once, sharply, then stalked rapidly up the hill, staking her cane in the ground in front of her.

Only Mo, Will, and Liesl were left.

"Well," Liesl said, feeling shy again.

"Well," Will said, shifting his weight uncomfortably.

"Well," Mo said cheerfully, looking from Will to Liesl, and back to Will. "Warm out, isn't it?" He removed his hat.

Will and Liesl nodded. They were feeling too timid to speak.

"I suppose it's too warm for hot chocolate," Mo said thoughtfully. A new idea had worked itself into his brain.

Those kids look like they could use some taking care of. Yes. Two lost children, about the same age as Bella was when she disappeared. A nice hot meal; a change of clothes; a place to lie down. Out loud he said, "But maybe some chocolate milk. Yes, I think chocolate milk would be nice. Don't you?"

Will and Liesl looked at each other and smiled. They bobbed their heads vigorously.

"Good. Very good." Just like that, Mo's already enormous heart expanded even more, enough to enclose the two children and hold them safely there forever.

(And this, really, is the story-within-the-story, because if you do not believe that hearts can bloom suddenly bigger, and that love can open like a flower out of even the hardest places, then I am afraid that for you the road will be long and brown and barren, and you will have trouble finding the light.

But if you *do* believe, then you already know all about magic.)

"Come on, then," Mo said, and called for Lefty, who shot a last, regretful look at the very clever butterfly and came trotting back to Mo, to be settled in her sling.

Will and Liesl walked very close together, with their fingers barely touching. Mo placed a hand on Will's shoulder, kindly.

"Why do you call her Lefty?" Will asked as they walked up the hill: Mo, Lefty, Will, and Liesl.

"That's a good question," Mo said, "and it's a funny story. I never was any good at leaving people to their own business, you know. Mrs. Elkins—that's my landlady, you'll meet her soon enough—is always telling me to mind my beeswax. . . ."

And so Mo spoke, and Will and Liesl listened, and Lefty purred, and the sun shone.

They passed the place where Liesl's house had once been. Out of the ash, she knew, flowers would grow.

She spelled the word *ineffable* in her head, just once.

AUTHOR'S NOTE

I wrote *Liesl & Po* during a concentrated two-month period. It was different from anything else I had ever written; I didn't know what it would be, or whether it would be anything. I certainly didn't think it would be publishable.

I knew only that I needed to write it. At the time, I was dealing with the sudden death of my best friend. The lasting impact of this loss reverberated through the months, and it made my world gray and murky, much like the world Liesl inhabits at the start of the story. The idea for the book came from a fantasy I entertained during those months: I dreamed about unearthing my friend's ashes from the decorative wall in which they'd been interred and scattering them over the water, the only place he'd ever felt truly at peace.

And so my fantasies were transformed into the figure of a little girl who embarks on a journey not just to restore the ashes of a loved one to a peaceful place but to restore color and life to a world that has turned dim and gray.

Only in retrospect did I realize that I was writing about myself—that Liesl's journey was my own. *Liesl & Po* is the most personal book I've ever written, and even though it takes place at an unspecified time in an unspecified place and features magic and alchemists and ghosts, it is a confessional.

Additionally, *Liesl & Po* is the embodiment of what writing has always been for me at its purest and most basic—not a paycheck, certainly; not an idea, even; and not an escape. Actually, it is the opposite of an escape; it is a way back *in*, a way to enter and make sense of a world that occasionally seems harsh and terrible and mystifying.

And, of course, it is a way of finding a happy ending— even, or especially, when the happy ending is denied me in real life. Let it be an escape for its readers. For me, it is a way of not letting go.

This book means a tremendous amount to me. And I hope it has meant something to you, too.

LAUREN OLIVER

LAUREN OLIVER's first novel was the *New York Times* bestseller *Before I Fall*, a *Publishers Weekly* Best Book of the Year. She followed that up with her thrilling *Delirium*, which debuted on the *New York Times* bestseller list and is the first book in a trilogy. *Liesl & Po* is Lauren's first novel for younger readers. A graduate of the University of Chicago and New York University's MFA program, she lives in Brooklyn, New York. Lauren is also the co-owner of Paper Lantern Lit, a book development company. You can visit her online at www.laurenoliverbooks.com and on Twitter, Facebook, and MySpace.

KEI ACEDERA

KEI ACEDERA is the art director and co-owner of Imaginism Studios. She is known for her imaginative character designs for Tim Burton's *Alice in Wonderland* and for her illustrations for bestselling children's books, including Alec Greven's *How to Talk to Girls*. Kei's designs will be featured in upcoming films with Sony, Warner Bros., and Universal Studios. You can visit her online at www.imaginismstudios.com.

First published in United States of America by HarperCollins Children's Books,
a division of HarperCollins Publishers

First published in Great Britain in 2011 by Hodder & Stoughton
An Hachette UK company

First published in paperback in 2012

1

Text copyright © 2011 by Laura Schechter
Illustrations copyright © 2011 by Kei Acedera

A CIP catalogue record for this title is available from the British Library.

Paperback ISBN 978 1 444 72310 6
Ebook ISBN 978 1 444 72309 0

Printed and bound by Clays Ltd, St Ives plc.

Hodder & Stoughton policy is to use papers that are natural, renewable
and recyclable products and made from wood grown in sustainable forests.
The logging and manufacturing processes are expected to conform to the
environmental regulations of the country of origin.

Hodder & Stoughton Ltd
338 Euston Road
London NW1 3BH

www.hodder.co.uk

LIESL & PO
A Reading Group Guide

1. How is Po different from how you would imagine a ghost to be?

2. What does Po hate about the impression living people have of ghosts?

3. What do you imagine it is like on the Other Side? Is what you imagine different from what Po describes?

4. Why is 'ineffable' Liesl's favourite word? What is your favourite word? What is it about the word that makes it your favourite?

5. Why wouldn't Liesl's stepmother let Liesl see her father to say good-bye before he died? How would you describe the way Liesl's stepmother treats her?

6. How is Will treated by the alchemist? How is the way Will is treated similar to how Liesl is treated by her stepmother?

7. What does Will remember about Kevin Donnell's house when looking at Liesl in her attic window?

8. How does Will's decision to first make the delivery to Mr. Gray prove to be a fateful one?

9. What are Mr. Gray's profession and his side business?

10. Why are people starving all across the world?

11. What are the '*feelings and attachments long forgotten*' that Liesl stirs up in Po (p.72)?

12. How does Po meet Liesl's father? What do you think Henry means when he says, '*It was the soup, you know. I should never have eaten the soup*' (p.81)? What was Henry and Augusta's marriage like?

13. What does Augusta fear Liesl will be able to do with the magic powder?

14. Why does Liesl run away from Will? What makes Will think that Liesl might be crazy?

15. What does Augusta confess to Liesl?

16. What does Liesl realize when she gets to the Red House?

17. Why does seeing her house consumed by fire make Liesl feel joy and relief?

18. What happens when the true meaning of the magic is revealed: '*The dead will rise from glade to glen and ancient will be young again*' (p.288)? What is Liesl able to do?

19. What happens when Po and Bundle turn golden?

20. What do you think will become of Liesl and Will?

Liesl & Po

LAUREN OLIVER

To hear the official *Liesl & Po* song,
Train With Wings, and for more
exclusive content visit

www.lieslandpo.com

For all the latest news about Lauren Oliver
and her books visit

www.laurenoliverbooks.com

THE
SPINDLERS

When Liza's brother, Patrick, changes overnight, Liza knows exactly what has happened: the spindlers have got to him, and stolen his soul. She knows, too, that she is the only one who can save him.

To rescue Patrick, Liza must go Below, armed with little more than her wits and a broom. There, she uncovers a vast world populated with talking rats, music-loving moles, greedy troglods, and overexcitable nids . . . as well as strange monsters and terrible dangers. But she will face her greatest challenge at the spindlers' nests, where she encounters the evil Queen and must pass a series of deadly tests – or else her soul, too, will remain Below forever.

Coming September 2012

CHAPTER ONE

The Changeling, and the Letters Spelled in Cereal

One night when Liza went to bed, Patrick was her chubby, stubby, candy-grubbing, and pancake-loving younger brother, who irritated her and amused her both, and the next morning, when she woke up, he was not.

She could not describe the difference. He looked the same, and was wearing the same pair of ratty space-alien pyjamas, with the same fat toe sticking out of the hole in the left foot of his red socks, and he came down the stairs exactly the same way the real Patrick would have done: *bump*, *bump*, *bump*, sliding on his rump.

But he was not the same.

In fact, he was quite, quite different.

It was something in the way he looked at her: it was as though someone had reached behind his eyes and wrung away all the sparkle, leaving only a blank gaze. He walked quietly – too quietly – to the table, sat nicely in his chair, and placed a napkin on his lap.

The real Patrick never used a napkin.

Nobody else noticed a thing. Mrs. Elston, Liza's mother, continued sorting through the stack of bills on the kitchen table, making occasional noises of unhappiness. Liza's father continued passing in and out of the room, his tie unknotted and wearing only one sock, muttering distractedly to himself.

The fake-Patrick picked up his spoon and gave Liza a look that chilled her to her very centre.

Then the fake-Patrick began to eat his cereal, methodically, slowly, fishing all the alphabet letters out of his Alpha-Bits one by one and lining them up along the rim of his bowl.

Liza's heart sank. She knew, at that moment, what had happened, as well as she knew that the sky was up and the ground was down and if you turned around fast enough in a circle and then stood still, the world would keep turning the circle for you.

Patrick's soul had been taken by the spindlers. And they had left this thing, this not-younger-brother, in its place.

"Mom," she said, and then, when her mother did not immediately respond, tried again a little louder. "Mom."

"Mmm?" Mrs. Elston jumped. She squinted at Liza

for a moment, the same way she had looked at the instruction sheet that came along with the Easy-Assemble Coffee Table in Mahogany, the one she had had to return to the store after she could not figure out how to screw the legs on.

"Patrick's being weird," Liza said.

Mrs. Elston stared blankly at her daughter. Then she whirled around, suddenly, to her husband. "Did you ever pay the electric bill?"

Mr. Elston didn't seem to hear her. "Have you seen my glasses?" he asked, lifting the fruit bowl and peering underneath it.

"They're on your head."

"Not *those* glasses. My reading glasses."

Mrs. Elston sighed. "It says this is our final notice. I don't remember a first notice. Didn't we pay the electric bill? I could have sworn . . ."

"I can't go to work without my glasses!" Mr. Elston opened the refrigerator, stared at its contents, closed the refrigerator, and rushed out of the room.

Across the table, the fake-Patrick began rearranging the cereal letters on the outside of his bowl. He spelled out three words: I H-A-T-E Y-O-U. Then he folded his hands and stared at her with that strangely vacant look, as though the black part of his eyes had eaten up all the color.

Liza's insides shivered again. She slid off her chair and went over to her mother. She tugged at the sleeve of her mother's nightgown, which had a small coffee stain at its elbow. "Mommy."

"Yes, princess?" she asked distractedly.

"Patrick's freaking me out."

"Patrick," Mrs. Elston said, without looking up from her notepad, on which she was now scribbling various figures. "Stop bothering your sister."

Here's what the real Patrick would have done: he would have stuck out his tongue, or thrown his napkin at Liza in retaliation, or he would have said, "It's her *face* that's the bother."

But this impostor did none of those things. The impostor just stared quietly at Liza and smiled. His teeth looked very white.

"Mom—" Liza insisted, and her mother sighed and threw down her pencil with so much force that it bounced.

"*Please*, Liza," she said, with barely concealed impatience. "Can't you see that I'm busy? Why don't you go outside and play for a bit?"

Liza went outside. It was a hot and hazy morning — far too hot for late April. She was hoping to see one of the neighbours out doing something – watering a plant, walking a dog – but it was very still. Liza almost never saw the neighbours. It was not that kind of neighbourhood. She didn't even know most of their names: only Mrs. Costenblatt, who was so old she looked exactly like a prune.

Today, as on most days, Mrs. Costenblatt was sitting on her porch, rocking, and fanning herself with one of the Chinese delivery menus that were often stuck — mysteriously, invisibly, in the middle of the night — under the front door.

"Hello," she called out to Liza, and waved.

"Hello," Liza called back. She liked Mrs. Costenblatt, even though Mrs. Costenblatt hardly ever moved except to rock in her chair, and could not be counted on to do anything interesting.

"Would you like a glass of lemonade?" Mrs. Costenblatt called out. "Or a cookie?" She offered Liza lemonade and a cookie every time they saw each other, unless it was winter, in which case she offered hot chocolate and a cookie. Mrs. Costenblatt liked to rock even in cold weather, and she would appear on her porch so bundled in blankets and scarves, she looked like an overstuffed coatrack.

"Not today, thank you," Liza said regretfully, as she always did. She was not allowed to accept things to eat or drink from Non-Family Members. Liza often wished the rule applied to Family Members instead. She would much rather have had one of Mrs. Costenblatt's cookies than her aunt Virginia's tuna casserole.

She wondered whether she should tell Mrs. Costenblatt about Patrick, but decided against it. Two weeks earlier, at recess, when she had tried to tell Christina Millicent and Emma Wong about the spindlers and the constant threat they posed, they had laughed at her and called her a liar. Mrs. Costenblatt was a good listener – partly, Liza thought, because she couldn't hear very well – but Liza didn't want to risk it.

There was only one thing that Liza hated more than liars, and that was being accused of being one.

At one edge of the yard, a pile of pinecones had been neatly stacked. Liza had arranged them this way only yesterday, thinking that she and Patrick might play a round of Pinecone Bowling in the morning. But of course she could not play with the false Patrick; he would no doubt find a way to cheat.

She had a sudden, wrenching, fierce desire that Anna, her old babysitter, would come home. She would have played Pinecone Bowling. In fact, she had invented it.

Last fall Anna had gone away to college, which meant that she had moved and couldn't babysit anymore, and instead Liza and Patrick were left with Mandy, who always chewed her gum too loudly and didn't like to play games – she didn't like anything, really, except talking on the phone. Anna had come over to babysit several times over Christmas, but on her spring break she had gone away with her friends. Liza and Patrick had gotten a water-warped postcard from her, but most of the writing had been too blurry to read.

In addition to the postcard she had sent from the beach, she had sent two letters from college, and a white sweatshirt with a fierce-looking bear on the front, explaining in the attached note that it was her school's mascot. Patrick had cried like a baby when it turned out the sweatshirt was in Liza's size, and she had finally lent it to him. He had promptly spilled tomato sauce on it, and she'd refused to speak to him for an entire day.

Liza knew it was stupid, but sometimes she fantasized that Anna would turn up again and confess to her deepest secret: that Liza and Patrick were, in fact, her siblings, and they had all been torn apart by some horrible event when they were little and forced into different families.

Liza's fantasies were a little hazy after that point, but she thought that somehow she, Anna, and Patrick would end up on a long journey together, hunting down some of the magical creatures Anna had always told them about, like gnomes and nimphids (who were beautiful but bad-tempered).

Wind rustled the trees, and then everything was still again.

Liza sighed. Anna would also have known what to do about the spindlers; she was, after all, the person who had first told Liza and Patrick about them. She was the one who had warned them about the strange spider creatures and had told them what they must do to be protected.

Liza scanned the yard for gnomes, but saw nothing. Only last week, Patrick – the real Patrick – had spotted one scampering into the rhododendron.

"Look, Liza!" he had cried out, and she had turned just in time to see a hard, brown hide, which was as cracked and weathered as the brown leather purse her mom had had since *she* went to college.

It was too hot for the gnomes today, Liza decided. Anna had told Liza they preferred cool climates.

Liza pressed her face up against the small fir tree that stood next to the birdbath, inhaling deeply. It was easier to see the magic through its branches, she found. The scratchy needles poked deeply into her skin, and she stood and squinted through the layers of green. Looking at the world through the fir tree meant seeing only the essential things: the vivid green of the grass, dew glistening on petals, a robin flicking its tail, a squirrel rustling through the rhododendron, a miracle of life and growth that forever pulsed under the ordinariness.

And, of course, it was only when looking through the tree that you could make a wish and have it come true – Anna had also told them that.

Liza spoke a wish quietly into the scratchy branches.

We will not repeat it. Everyone knows that only wishes that are kept secret will ever come true. But know this: the wish was about Patrick.

Look out for the novel in September 2012.

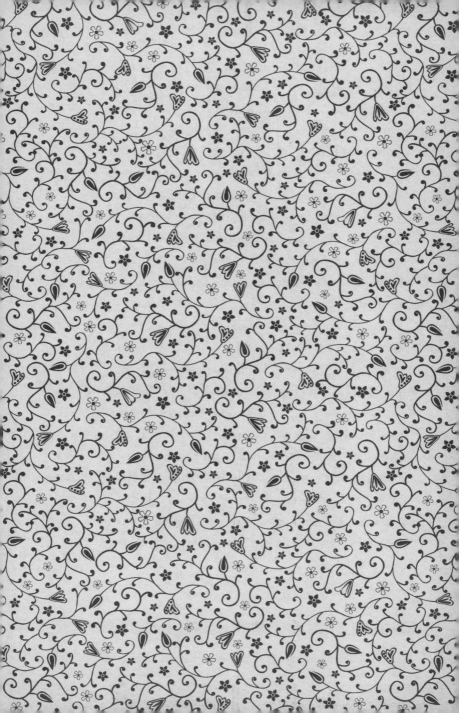

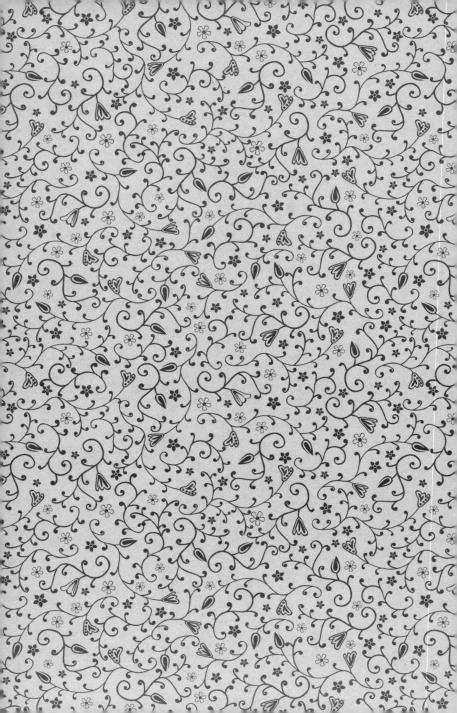